THE LOVE
OF
HIGHLAND MARY

THE LOVE
OF
HIGHLAND MARY

JESS BOLTON

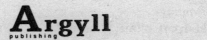

© Jess Bolton 1994

Published by
Argyll Publishing
Glendaruel
Argyll PA22 3AE

**British Library Cataloguing-in-
Publication Data.
A catalogue record for this book is
available from the British Library.**

ISBN 1 874640 01 7

Typeset and origination
Cordfall Ltd, 041 332 4640

Printing
HarperCollins, Glasgow

How sweetly bloomed the gay green birk
How rich the hawthorn's blossom,
As underneath their fragrant shade
I clasped her to my bosom!
The golden hours, on angel wings,
Flew o'er me and my dearie,
For dear to me, as light and life,
Was my sweet Highland Mary.

from *Highland Mary*
    written in 1792, six years after her death

Acknowledgements

For giving their time, their interest and their encouragement during the writing of this book, my grateful thanks are due to all of the following.

My publisher, Derek Rodger; Mr Bill Scott, Head Librarian Kirn Archives Library and staff; Mr G Roy, Bookpoint Dunoon and Greenock; the Campbell family of Dunoon, Hamish, Margart and Emma; Mr and Mrs Allan and all members of the Dunoon Heritage Trust; the staff of Dunoon Library; Mrs C Hutcheson, Milton House; Mr Bill McKissock, Mr Barry White, the ladies of the committee and the Rev Mr Stewart of St John's church, Dunoon; Mr Bob Peat of the Greenock Burns Club (the Mother Club); Mrs Cooper-White, Head Librarian the McLean Library; Joy Menteith, Head Librarian Greenock and Inverclyde; the staff of Gourock Library; the Mitchell Library; the Paisley Library and Museum; the Scottish Record Office, Edinburgh; Mr E McGilp; Mrs C Telfer; Mr Peter Westwood of Paisley; Mr Peter Bolton, Christine and Laura; Mr T Lang and family; Mr and Mrs J Gilmour; Mr and Mrs J Alder; and many others whose names I do not know.

Jess Bolton
Gourock , September 1994

Contents

Preface

My Highland lassie was a warm-hearted,
charming young creature as ever blessed a
man with her love.

Burns MS

Much has been written, down the years, of the love that
Robert Burns, the national Bard of Scotland, had for the
woman who came to be known as Highland Mary. He
wrote lines in her name; she is mentioned in his letters;
and after their deaths, among all of Burns' women, the
name of Mary Campbell has held the most fascination
and enjoyed the most prominence. Statues have been
erected of her in her birthplace in Dunoon, in Liverpool
and in New York.

All of this attention is premised on Burns' love for
Mary. It is in the nature of much of the mythology that
surrounds the poet and his life, that not much has
appeared in print about the love of Mary Campbell for
Burns. As the title of this book suggests, it is hoped that
this imbalance is now set right.

Certainly much observation and comment on the
life and loves of Robert Burns is intemperate – as uneven
and impulsive and reckless as the poet himself is widely
imagined to have been. Burns' sexual appetite, for
example, is the stuff of legend. One recent newspaper

article famously continued the myth-making, alleging that during his time there, the face of Robert Burns could be seen in every pram in Edinburgh's Princes Street. A rake and a lad!

His drinking prowess and social behaviour is imagined to have been excessive – in his lifetime he was considered a "drunken dissipated character". Commentators wrote of the poet as possessing certain personal "frailties". Even before he had departed this earth in 1796, Robert Burns was, in his own land, already categorised as the wayward genius.

Just how a man of such voracious sexual hunger, such an appetite for strong drink and of such an impulsive disposition could cope with life, far less achieve prominence through producing a considerable body of fine and enduring work, the modern reader is left to wonder. When placed on top of the other mundane but no less onerous tasks in his short life – variously running a farm, his work as an Exciseman which involved miles of horseback riding and careful record-keeping every week, his fathering of nine children to his wife, Jean Armour – we moderns can only marvel that they don't make then like that any more!

Given this stylised and rather cultish view of the Bard, what hope a credible interpretation of the women in his life? Rather than just a recipient of Burns' affections, Mary Campbell was of course, a person in her own right – a woman, with a personal history, a life and feelings of her own, and a perspective rooted in her time, place and class.

She was born, Mairi Campbell, the first child of Archibald and Agnes Campbell, in a cottage on the farm of Auchamore near Dunoon in Argyll in 1763. The appellation, Highland relates to the physical and human geography of her origins. Then as now, the settlement of Dunoon was a mere three miles across the River Clyde estuary from the Central Lowlands of Scotland. Geologically, culturally and in the language spoken, especially in the eighteenth century, it lies a good bit further distant. In contrast to the Scots and English tongue a few miles to the south, Argyll at this time was almost entirely Gaelic speaking. Mary was the Scots or Anglicised version of Mairi.

Archibald and Agnes are likely to have crofted some land at Auchamore, but Archibald had a more regular and lucrative source of income as a Captain of a small cargo vessel which plied the west coast waters. At some point during their eldest daughter's early childhood Captain Campbell moved his family to Kintyre.

When of an age (probably around 12 or 13), as was common for girls of "decent" families, Mary went into service. And for a few years she was nursemaid to the family of the minister at Lochranza on the nearby Isle of Arran.

Later, through family contacts she procured another service posting in the kitchen of the Montgomerie household at Coilsfield in Ayrshire. It was while working here that she was to come in contact with the young Robert Burns of nearby Mossgiel farm.

She was to move on to the household of Gavin Hamilton, a patron of Burns and sponsor of his first and famous Kilmarnock edition of poems. At around this time, in early 1785 Burns' liaison with the woman who was to become his wife and the mother of many of his children, Jean Armour, was becoming fraught. Her family took none too kindly to the freethinking poet with a reputation as a womaniser. Worse, Jean was with child.

Events at this time in the life of Robert Burns were

moving rapidly. It is thought that he and Mary Campbell separated, but not before tenderly exchanging Bibles and making a solemn promise of betrothal. (These bibles still exist and are preserved in the Burns Monument Museum in Alloway.) By the following year, Burns was published, his literary career was taking off, he appeared to have abandoned his plans to migrate to the West Indies and he had married Jean Armour. And in a tragic development, he had lost his Highland Mary.

On the way to Glasgow from Kintyre, it is thought to take up another position in the service of a Colonel McIvor, while staying in the household of a cousin of her mother, in Charles Street Greenock, she contracted typhoid fever and on or around 21st October 1786, Mary Campbell died. She would be just 23 years old.

She was buried in Greenock's Old West Kirkyard, in a plot of ground recently acquired by the husband of the same relative, Peter McPherson. Her grave was unmarked until 25th January 1842, when a foundation stone was laid for the erection of a suitable Monument, paid for by admirers of Robert Burns, as a tribute to his lost love.

Some years later, when due to expansion of the Caird & Co (later Harland & Wolff) shipyard at Greenock, the Old West Kirk moved to another site, the remains were exhumed and removed to Greenock Cemetery, where they were given a second and full ceremonial burial on 13th November 1920. There lies Mary Campbell to this day.

A simple enough story perhaps, of the short life of a simple, straightforward and ordinary Highland lass. But in the scramble to interpret and contain the life of no less an acquaintance that a national Bard, nothing is ever simple. Mary Campbell's life has been dissected in turn.

Her presence has been held to be everything from a mere episode (one among many feminine distractions) in the life of Burns, to the one true, pure and unfulfilled love of his life.

In the otherwise thorough and balanced Saltire Award-winning biography *Burns* (1992) by scholar James Mackay, Highland Mary is held to be "almost entirely the invention of the nineteenth century myth-makers."

"In the cult of Burns," writes Mackay, "Highland Mary assumed the role of the Blessed Virgin."

Yet the controversy is not dead. One enduring source of debate, for instance, concerns the findings of the grave diggers when Mary Campbell's remains were exhumed from the Old West Kirkyard in 1920. At the foot of Mary's coffin was found an old oak casket containing the bones of a newborn infant.

Even to Mary sceptics like Mackay, this is a matter of high intrigue. The invention of Victorian romanticists or not, Mackay floats the notion of calling in the grave diggers yet again (and the forensic scientists) to exhume the "rickle o' banes" that are the infant remains and to do a DNA testing against easily accessible relics of Burns. Just to settle the controversy!

Another source of debate about Highland Mary concerns her integrity and standards of sexual propriety. According to one set of papers held by Edinburgh University Library, Mary Campbell's character was "loose in the extreme". It is said she was "kept" for some time by a Captain James Montgomery and an account is given, anecdotal certainly, of an amorous encounter between the two in a room at the alehouse in Mauchline, around the time when Mary was in the employ of the Hamilton household.

At this, two centuries distance of time, what is to be

made of the evidence? What seems clear is that in the affairs of Robert Burns, matters of the heart are discussed in any rational way, only with difficulty. Much of the fascination in prolonging a discussion about a young woman's sexuality and attraction for a man does seem frankly prurient, the preoccupation perhaps of repressed Victorian moralists. As with the Bard himself, much of a reading of the critics on these matters has a certain projective quality. Practically without exception, all of these commentators on Burns' life and loves have been men.

Jess Bolton has researched original records and has pieced together an engaging story which addresses the points of contention in understanding Burns' relationship with this, till now, rather shadowy figure. Jess Bolton brings a female perspective to Mary Campbell's life and a historian's insight to the life of the time, particularly the vision of the world that might have prevailed in the mind of a young female Gael.

Is the decision by a local author, to write up her research in the manner of a kind of historical detective story, valid? And can the decision to issue the book by an Argyll publisher be seen as more to do with commercial opportunism than a search for truth? These questions are, of course, for the reader to judge.

Burns does seem to have had a devotion to the memory of Mary Campbell. He was known to be haunted by remorse for years after Mary's death. What love does a man remember perhaps most of all, if not that love that was never fulfilled?

The Publisher
Argyll, September 1994

CHAPTER 1

A Birth at Auchamore

Golden dawn was breaking over the little cottage of Auchamore, as a new-born baby's cry joined the first hesitant bird-song. Inside, the young mother reached out to take her child into her arms. The long hours of her labour were forgotten as she gazed at the rose-petal face, the soft dark hair, the tiny perfect hands.

The midwife, well-pleased at bringing such a bonnie bairn into the world, looked on, asking, "Well now, Mistress Campbell, is it pleased you are with your daughter, or were you looking for a son?

Agnes Campbell lifted her head, eyes shining like stars. "Pleased? Such a poor word to tell you what I feel this moment, when my heart is so full of love. I will have other children, God willing, and they will be dear to me, but none so dear as this, my first born girl-child."

Tenderly she lifted the baby's hand and laughed when she felt it curl tightly around her finger. "Look, Mistress Lindsay, how strong she is! and she has the look of her Father. She is going to be a black Campbell!"

Rachael Lindsay shook her head "No, my dear, this little one will take after you, with your bonnie golden hair."

Agnes Campbell stared at the Midwife and said

incredulously, "but her hair is black as soot."

"Yes, but see you," she bent over the sleeping babe and traced the line of the eyebrows and Agnes Campbell saw that they were dusted with gold, as were the curling lashes.

Mrs Lindsay continued, "In a few weeks the black will be gone and she'll have your colouring".

"Och, Mrs Lindsay, that surely will please my man! He's had his heart set on a lass, as he said, 'just like her Mother'."

"And have you a name for her?"

"Aye, we have. She is to be named Mairi, after my GrandMother".

"And when is Captain Campbell's boat due to arrive?"

"Tomorrow, as fast as he can sail from Bute."

Her voice broke into a sigh, a mingling of anticipation and weariness and the midwife quickly removed the sleeping infant. She placed her in the newly-made wooden cradle, between the soft linen covers and turned to her patient. Before she could speak, a sound broke the morning silence . . . the clear ringing of a church bell.

Agnes Campbell opened her eyes and murmured, "I had forgotten this was the Sabbath. Someone must tell the Minister of Mairi's birth, so that she might receive his blessing."

Sleep overcame her, and she did not hear Mrs Lindsay say, "Don't you fret, lass, your bairn will be blessed, and she will be a blessing to you and your man. Of that I am sure."

Gently she rocked the cradle, gazing down at the babe sleeping so peacefully, with one tiny hand spread starlike on the cover.

Next morning, Archie Campbell made fast his boat in Dunoon Bay, said his goodbyes to his Mate and set off to climb the green Castle Hill, beyond which lay his home.

Anxious as he was to see his Agnes and for news of her health, he couldn't help stopping at the top of the hill for a sight of the river.

It stretched out under the deep blue sky, smooth as silk, and Archie Campbell drew a deep breath of thankfulness as he murmured his gratitude to God for giving him safe passage home and asked a blessing on his wife and their coming child. He gathered a handful of sweet scented wild flowers, red and white clover, long stemmed yellow buttercups and white daisies. He wrapped their stems in cool burdock leaves to keep them fresh for, unusual in a man, he shared his wife's love of plants and flowers, and liked to see them on the window sill and table.

As he strode over the far side of the hill into the meadows, he caught sight of his cottage, pale smoke curling from the chimney, door wide open to the sun. Archie Campbell was never to forget the sight that met his eyes as he entered his house that sunlit May day. His Agnes was sitting up in bed, and in her arms was their babe. Transfixed for a moment, he crossed the room and, kneeling, enfolded his wife and child in his arms, too deeply moved to speak.

Agnes Campbell whispered, "Well, husband, do you not want to know whether 'tis a son or a daughter I have to give you?"

He lifted his head and gently, reverently, he kissed her soft lips before taking his first look at his child. The sleeping eyes opened, blue as the sky, and seemed to study him gravely. Timorously, he touched the tiny face, laughing aloud as the pink lips parted in a yawn.

"I think our first-born is a daughter. Too beautiful she is to be a boy! Am I right, my Agnes?"

Smiling with happiness, she answered him. "Yes, you are right. This is our daughter, Mairi Campbell, born yesterday morning and very happy she is to be meeting her Father."

Now, Archie Campbell presented his wife with the nosegay of wild flowers which he still clutched and, unwrapping the burdock leaves, he selected a pink and white daisy which he placed in his new daughter's tiny hand, saying, "Thou art more lovely than this flower of Spring, my dearest little babe, and already there is a look on you of your Mother."

At this moment, the Midwife came in, and cried, "Captain Campbell, have you clean lost your wits? The child will eat the flower and choke on it."

Guiltily, Archie removed the daisy from Mairi's clutching fingers and reached for his Seaman's bag. Rummaging inside, he drew out a string of five silver bells, which tinkled musically as he moved them "Well now, my dear Mrs Lindsay, if I fasten these bells to the little one's cradle will they meet with your approval?"

Agnes Campbell cried out with pleasure, "Oh, but how lovely they are! Where did you find them?"

"I purchased them from a sailor on a trading ship. He told me they were fashioned in a little village high up on a French mountain, and I knew they would please our baby."

Again, he reached into the bag, saying, "And these velvet ribbons are for your hair, lass, blue to match your eyes."

Rachael Lindsay smiled at him. "Och, it is a thoughtful man you are, Mr Campbell. And now, take hold of your little maid, while I make your wife presentable for her visitors".

"Ah, but Mistress Lindsay, first of all I would wish to thank you from my heart for your great kindness in caring for Agnes, and for bringing our daughter safe into the world. You would honour me by accepting this gift" and he handed her a shawl of finest wool, brown with deep fringes and bordered with cream roses.

Rachael Lindsay, speechless, took it into her hands and, stroking its softness with a gentle finger, she shook her head at him. "Mr Campbell I do thank you, it is beautiful, but it troubles me to think of you spending your hard-earned money on such a gift for me".

Archie Campbell reassured her. "No money did I give, Mistress. For this, I exchanged a pair of fine leather shoes, given to me by John the Saddler in return for my help with his work. and I have brought him orders for more. Now can I hold the babe, while you help Agnes?"

For only a second did Archie Campbell feel awkward, as he held the tiny form of his child then his love overcame him and he cradled his daughter in the crook of his arm, and hummed an old Gaelic lullaby till her eyes closed in sleep.

In a short time, the midwife freshened up her patient and dressed her in a fine white cotton shift, edged at the neck with lace, placing over it a knitted shawl in shaded blue, next she plaited the soft, golden hair, working into it the velvet ribbons, fastening the braids into a coronet on the top of her head.

Standing back to admire her handiwork, she said with satisfaction, "There now, Mistress Campbell, you're as pretty as a picture. Now I'm going to leave you with your man and your bairn. There's broth on the fire, and bread new-baked and see you make a good meal and drink plenty of milk for the babe. I'll be back in two hours to let in your visitors. They will keep you company while the men join Mr Campbell at the Inn, to drink the health of Miss Mairi Campbell.

CHAPTER 2
Changing Winds

The years had been kind to Agnes Campbell, and as she stood at the door of Auchamore Cottage, she appeared little changed from the early days of her Marriage. Still slender, with shining hair plaited around her head, she shaded her eyes from the glare of the sun as she looked for her two eldest children.

Since Mairi's birth ten years earlier, she had borne three others; a black-haired son, Robert, nicknamed "Rab-the-Pirate"; a brown-haired girl, Agnes; and lastly another black-haired boy named Archibald for his Father.

The sound of voices reached her from the back of the barn, Mary's voice, remonstrating, defiantly answered by Rab.

"Come down at once, Rab, or it is trouble you will be in for upsetting the hay."

"I will not, then, and you can't make me!"

His Mother swiftly rounded the corner and saw Mairi gazing up at the haystack where Rab was standing, hands on hips, glaring down at her.

Agnes Campbell spoke quietly, but with an inflection that brooked no denial, "Robert Campbell, you will do what your sister tells you." The boy's bravado was instantly squashed and docilely he slid to the ground.

His Mother pointed to the scattered stalks lying in untidy heaps. "You will gather in all of Mr Campbell's hay and then you will go and tell him it is sorry you are for being such a wicked boy. This hay is needed till the new grass begins, and shame on you for wasting it."

Mairi bent to help him, her kind heart moved to compassion by the quiver of her brother's lip and his downcast eyes.

Agnes Campbell went on, "If you are quick and work well, I will allow Mairi to take you to visit your Uncle Donald to see his new baby goats, but you must be deserving of such a treat." Mairi laughed to see how quickly her brother threw off his gloom and she could hardly keep up with him as they gathered in the loose hay and replaced it on the depleished stack.

Before they set off, Agnes Campbell looked them over, and nodded her approval; Mairi, tall for her ten years and Rab, two years her junior, catching up fast in height. So different in nature, she reflected, sunny-tempered Mairi with her happy outlook, always the peacemaker, ever-ready to help with the younger children or run errands for the neighbours - nothing was a trouble to her; and Rab, a wild, steering laddie, always rebelling against "petticoat rule" but possessing a tender heart for small, helpless animals and, hidden though it was, a love for parents and siblings. His nickname of "Rab the-Pirate" came from his fiercely avowed intention to make piracy his career, after listening to his Father's stirring tales of Captain Kidd and Bluebeard.

In a fever of impatience to be off to his Uncle Donald, Rab fidgeted under his Mother's scrutiny as she warned him. "Now then, Robert Campbell, you will heed your sister and not be up to any of your tricks. Remember to cross the Baugie Burn by the little bridge, and not by the stones. Do you give me your promise?"

Dancing up and down as if he had hot coals under

his feet, reluctantly Rab gave his word. Mrs Campbell handed Mairi a basket containing fresh-baked oatmeal bannocks, a dish of home-churned butter and a round, yellow cheese, saying, "Tell Uncle Donald we will expect him for dinner on the Sabbath, when your Father will be home."

Mairi, carrying the basket in one hand, held tightly to Rab's hand with the other as they crossed the field.

Mairi Campbell, at the age of ten, possessed a maturity surpassing her years, and something in her Mother's last words troubled her. Why did she want Uncle Donald to visit on Sunday? Since her Father had bought a share in a coal-boat, he had had to spend more time at sea, delivering cargos to far-out islands and ports as far away as Campbeltown and when he was home, Sunday was a time for family, for stories from the Bible as they sat together round the fire. Her thoughts were interrupted by a tug on her hand as Rab pulled free and ran, shouting, down the hill.

Mairi, fleet of foot, soon caught up with him and beat him to the Baugie Burn. She stopped at the "bridge" a halved tree-trunk laid from one bank to the other with a rail on either side, and waited for Rab to reach her.

Panting, out of breath, he gazed longingly at the flat stones. "Look Mairi, the stones are safe, there's hardly any water today."

"Rab, you promised our Mother! See, I'll let you cross first over the bridge, if you give your word not to run."

"Och, all right, I will not run but I will walk as fast as I can." And suiting his actions to his words he was off, with Mairi close behind him.

A voice hailed them, "Greetings to you, Miss Mairi Campbell, and to you Master Robert. It is myself that has come to meet you and bid you welcome." Donald Campbell, known as 'Donald-of-the-Goats', was a small, thin man with a sparse ginger beard and red hair straggling onto his shoulders from under a faded blue bonnet. His kilt, of the Campbell tartan, hung loosely from his skinny hips, above his knees at the front, drooping at the back to touch his calves. As he leaned on his cromach, his odd appearance should have made him a figure of fun, but strangely, this was not so. About him was an aura of dignity, of authority, and his pale blue eyes had a piercing quality calculated to quell any familiarities.

Those eyes softened as they rested on his favourite niece, who curtseyed before him, saying shyly, "We thank you for your welcome, Uncle Donald, and bring you greetings from our Mother. You are bidden to sup with us on Sabbath, when our Father will be home. And see, Mother asks you to accept these small gifts." Donald Campbell patted Mairi's shining hair and relieved her of the basket, thanking her as graciously as if it contained gold and jewels.

Rab came forward and made his bow, gabbling out his greeting before asking, "Uncle Donald, where is Dainty? Why isn't he with you? And how many goat babies are there and what colour are they?"

As he ran out of breath, his uncle's eyes twinkled down at him. "Hush you now, Robert, till I sort out your words. First, Dainty has been left to guard the goats in my absence, that is why he is not at my side. And there are twelve kids, that being the proper name for young goats. The colours you will see for yourself."

With Mairi on one side and Rab on the other, he led them through the high grass to a little white house thatched with turf where two rowan trees arched over the door.

When their uncle led them round to the back yard, he was met by a bundle of black fur. Barking furiously, his Scottie dog Dainty launched itself at him, while he gentled it by touch and voice. "Whist now, whist ye, Dainty my man. Ye'll frighten the poor mothers out of their milk, then what will become of the younglins?"

Rab was almost speechless with delight as he tried to count the new kids, whose bleating made a fine din against the dog's barking and their Mothers agitated calls.

Mairi looked beseechingly at her uncle, who picked up a tiny animal with fleece of palest cream, and placed it in her arms.

The little head butted against her chin as it wriggled and bleated to get free, but Mairi's whispered words of endearment, her gentle hands stroking and caressing, quieted its fears. For a few seconds it nestled peacefully against her until the Mother, fearful for its safety, made a sudden rush, calling out loudly for her young. Carefully, Mairi lowered the little one to the ground. Laughing to see it stagger on unsteady legs to its Mother, butting her to nuzzle for its milk.

All too soon the afternoon was over and their uncle accompanied them as far as the Baugie Burn, Dainty rushing backwards and forwards at their feet. Mairi had no need to caution Rab not to run across the bridge, he had tired himself out with the goats and was grateful to hold his sister's hand while walking quietly at her side.

Once over the bridge Mairi turned to her uncle, knowing he would remain on watch until they were out of sight. She smiled to see Dainty crouched at his feet, black ears alert, red tongue lolling out as he gazed up at his master, ready to rush homeward whenever he was bid.

Standing at the door of her cottage, Agnes Campbell watched golden-haired Mairi and black-haired Rab walk hand-in-hand towards her.

At the sight of his Mother, Rab forgot his tiredness and rushed to tell her all his news. Clutching her apron, his words tumbling over one another, he cried, "Mother, Mother, Uncle Donald has twelve new kids, all different colours and one of them is coal-black and I liked it best and . . . "

Smiling Agnes Campbell placed a finger over her son's lips, saying indulgently, "Take a breath, Robert, you will have time enough to tell your adventures after we have had our meal."

Holding him close to her side, she reached out to place her arm around Mairi and as they went into the house, they smiled at one another over Rab's impatience to get on with his story.

That Sunday evening, Mairi lay in her bed beside her sleeping sister Agnes. Tired as she was she could not rest as she listened to the voices of her parents and her Uncle Donald. All through the meal, she had been aware of words held back, of glances exchanged which she could not understand, but which made her uneasy in her mind. Now she heard the name "Campbeltown" mentioned more than once and then a sentence spoken by her Father caused her to sit bolt upright, heart beating so furiously that she lost the sense of the last words . . . "I have found us a house in Campbeltown, in Dalintober . . . " then something about moving at Whitsuntide.

Suddenly Mairi lay down and pulled the covers over her head. She wished passionately that she had not overheard her Father's words, for she did not wish to leave Auchamore, ever.

CHAPTER 3

Goodbye to Auchamore

An early morning mist lay over the thatched roof of Auchamore, fogging the bushes and silvering the cobwebs. The grass was milky-white, cold and wet against unprotected ankles as neighbours gathered round the home of Agnes and Archie Campbell.

Everyone in the little community was astir, even although it was barely six o'clock. The men were helping Archie Campbell to load his furniture onto a cart, with much good-humoured banter while the women gave a hand to his wife as she packed linen and dishes into boxes.

Mairi, with the aid of her friend Janet, dressed the younger children, Agnes and Archie, while Rab escaped with the excuse that he was going to meet his Uncle Donald.

Thanks to her Father's thoughtfulness, Mairi's sadness at leaving Auchamore had been alleviated. He had gained permission from Janet's parents to allow her to spend the summer with them in Campbeltown and now the friends were full of excited plans.

"Tis lucky you are to be missing school on Monday, Mairi," sighed Janet.

Mairi shook her head. "Why Janet, I like school. You know that. It is only the English that muddles my wits and ties knots in my tongue! Numbers and reading are just fine, in the Gaelic!"

The girls laughed together and Agnes Campbell's face brightened to hear them. Looking at her, Rachael Lindsay said, "Aye, Mistress Campbell, we are all going to miss your Mairi. There's not one of us has not had cause to bless her; always ready to run errands, or help with the bairns and never a cross word out of her."

Another neighbour broke in, "She is as good as she is bonny, too good for this world, indeed."

"No!" Agnes Campbell replied, her soft voice unusually sharp, "You are never to say that! Mairi will be a blessing long after we are gone, God willing!"

The sound of the pipes brought a momentary silence, then the women and children hurried outside to join the men as the sound grew in volume. The kilted figure of Donald Campbell swung into view, his nephew Rab striding proudly along at his side to the rousing music of a Campbell marching song. The dog, Dainty, trotted sedately at his master's heels, with an occasional leap in the air and an excited yelp.

The onlookers cheered and clapped as the pipes wailed into silence and "Donald of the Goats" thankfully accepted his dram, brought to him by his sister Agnes.

When all the men had a glass in their hand, Donald Campbell solemnly gave them the toast. "Here's good health to Archie and Agnes Campbell and to their children, Mairi, Robert, Agnes and Archibald. Good health, good luck and God's blessing on you."

Repeating the toast, the men downed their whisky while the women passed round oaten bannocks, hard-boiled eggs and new-baked bread and cups of frothing milk for the children.

At last it was done. The horses were yoked to the carts, the last goodbyes said, the children silent.

When they reached the harbour, Rab had to be forcibly restrained from leaping to the ground before ever the horse was brought to a standstill. Mairi's restraining hand on his arm, and his Father's stern warning to behave, forced him to curb his excitement.

As the last box was taken from the cart to join the others on the boat, Donald Campbell turned to Mairi and handed her a rolled-up scroll saying, "This is to remind you of Auchamore, Mairi. But do not open it until you are out of sight of Castle Hill, when it will serve to comfort you."

Mairi looked at him, blue eyes filled with tears, then bowed her head to receive his blessing. Turning away to hide his emotion, Donald Campbell called the other children to him, and gave to each one a carved wooden model of a goat, to Rab's vociferous delight when he saw that his was a replica of the little black kid.

When Archie Campbell had settled his wife and family on board, he thanked the men for their help and, turning to his brother-in-law, took his hand in a firm grip as he said, "Donald, my heartfelt thanks to you for all your kindness, and when you come to Campbeltown I hope it will be for a long visit. Agnes will miss you sore, as I too and my children."

"When I find someone I can trust with my goats, then sure it is I will come. Now be off with you, man, and I will play you out."

As the boat's sail caught the breeze, Donald Campbell tuned up his pipes and the haunting music of a sad Jacobite lament followed the Campbell's as they bid goodbye to the scene under the shadow of the green hill.

Mairi, golden hair blowing in the wind, strained her eyes to the kilted figure of her uncle, and strained her ears to the song of the pipes, until both sight and sound were lost to her.

True to her promise, Mairi did not open her uncle's gift until she could no longer see Dunoon. Then, she untied the scroll and gasped with delight at the carefully drawn plan which depicted well-known scenes and places. There was the thatched cottage of Auchamore, with the tall pine trees looking down from the hilltop; there was the path down to the Baugie Burn with the bridge and the stepping stones; on the other side was his own little house with the goats all around it and there was Uncle Donald himself in his blue bonnet and drooping kilt, pipes over his shoulder and Dainty jumping up at him; there was the field of the Butts, under the old castle walls, where she and Rab had gone with their Father to explore the dungeons and listen to the tales of long-ago battles and murders; behind the castle, the school, with the Dominie ringing the bell as the children straggled in.

Agnes Campbell gazed over Mairi's shoulder and exclaimed with pleasure, "Why, Mairi, what a wonderful gift! Your Uncle Donald has surpassed himself."

Mairi nodded in silent agreement, and drew comfort from her 'picture' as her uncle had known she would.

Tired out by the day's activities, Mairi lay down on the thick blanket beside her sister Agnes and felt the motion of the boat rocking her gently from side-to-side. She placed her precious map beneath her pillow and fell asleep murmuring, like a lullaby, "Auchamore, Baugie Burn, Uncle Donald, Castle Campbell, Dunoon . . . "

Mairi woke next morning to find herself in Kilchattan Bay, Bute, where they had been anchored for the night. Much refreshed, Mairi was soon washed and dressed and ready to help her Mother with the children.

When they had breakfasted on eggs, bread and milk,

Mairi carried food and drink to her Father as he sat at the tiller. The early morning air was cool, with a mist on the shore, and Mairi looked around with interested eyes, asking, "Is it far we have to go to Campbeltown, Father?"

"Far enough, lass, far enough! Today, we have to deal with the currents of Garroch Head before we reach Loch Ranza, that's on the Isle of Arran. We'll anchor there tonight and tomorrow we will be in Campbeltown.

After Garroch Head, the voyage was smooth and uneventful until they reached Loch Ranza. There, although it was still early in the evening, the sun had disappeared in a haze of mist and rain, and the sea was grey and choppy. Captain Campbell dropped anchor and almost at once a small boat could be seen approaching from the shore.

As it came alongside, Archie Campbell threw a rope down to the man in black oilskins, calling, "Well, well, Donald Campbell, what have you done to the weather? Come you aboard, man, and we'll have a dram before we go ashore."

Red-bearded Donald was introduced to Agnes and the children and, much taken with them, he issued an invitation to Rab and Mairi to accompany their Father to Loch Ranza, to "stretch your legs" as he put it. Rab danced with delight, but Mairi looked down at the small boat tumbling about in the waves, and shuddered. Not all Rab's taunting cries of "Scaredy cat" moved her from her decision and she was glad of her Mother's support when she silenced Rab by telling him firmly to leave his sister alone, as she needed her assistance.

When her husband and Rab returned, Agnes Campbell was pleased to see they had brought back food to supplement their stores. There was a can of new milk, a large loaf of wheaten bread, a round white cheese and a joint of boiled mutton. Now, she thought with satisfaction, they would not arrive in Campbeltown hungry, but well-fed and ready to face whatever lay in front of them.

CHAPTER 4
Campbeltown

In the morning, Archie Campbell left Arran. With a rising sea-breeze, he sailed his boat up the narrow strait between Davaar and the coast of Kintyre. From then on, a long straight run took him from the Trench to the Bay of Kilkerran.

Warning his wife it was time to get the children ready, he made for the northern shore and dropped anchor at Dalintober, where a goodly number of people had gathered to welcome them; among them was his cousin Elizabeth, and her husband John McNeill, who were to be their neighbours in their new home in Saddell Street, Broombrae.

As Archie Campbell helped his family onto the pier, the watchers saw the fair-haired Mother followed by golden-haired Mairi, Rab, Agnes and little Archie. Only Rab out of them all had no trouble adjusting his legs to the solid ground. The others swayed as if still aboard the boat and clung to each other for support.

Elizabeth McNeill, a little, plump woman with rosy cheeks, hurried to help, crying out, "Welcome, Agnes, welcome to Dalintober! This must be Mairi. My, what a bonnie lass you are, and Rab and Agnes and the bairn must be Archie! Here, give him to me, for you look ready to drop."

Willing hands helped them into the wagon which

awaited them, and leaving the men to unload their possessions, they set off for Broombrae.

As the cart was drawn along by the sturdy brown pony, Mairi looked around her at the many houses they passed, gardens bright with flowers, staring in wonder at the little boats drawn up on the shore, with fishing nets stretched out to dry in the sun. She heard Elizabeth McNeill say, "Look, Mairi and Robert, look over there! That is your new school."

Mairi saw a long, low building enclosed by a white stone wall with an iron gate in the middle and asked timidly, "When does school begin, Mrs McNeill?"

"Och, not till next week, lassie, you will have plenty of time to get used to things before then, and it would please me to have you call me Aunt Elizabeth, as we're close enough related."

The pony turned up a hill-road at right angle to the main road and stopped at what appeared to be two thatched houses with a common entrance in the middle.

Agnes Campbell helped her youngest son to the ground where Elizabeth waited to catch him. When they were all out of the cart, she led them through the gate in the fence and smiled round at Agnes, saying kindly, "Come away in, Agnes. See, I'm here on the right and your house is to the left. We'll go to my place for a bite of food and a pot of tea while the men bring the furniture and set your house to rights."

Mairi and Rab were almost too excited to enjoy their meal of milk, bread and honey and as soon as they had finished, they slipped away to look at their house before the men arrived.

"It's so big!" Mairi exclaimed as they entered the main room where a fire burned in the range. Rab jumped up and down on the bare wooden floor, making enough noise to waken the dead, but quickly stopped when Mairi warned him his Father would hear him at the bottom of the hill.

His high spirits still unquenched, Rab dashed outside to explore the garden, leaving Mairi to inspect the rest of the house on her own. There was one large bedroom and two small ones, a big kitchen and a scullery with a stone sink and wooden shelves completed her new home and Mairi knew she would be happy here.

At that moment Rab erupted into the parlour, feet banging like drums, face scarlet with excitement as he shouted, "Mairi, our Mother says the men are here and you've to take me and Agnes and Archie out to the garden and keep us there until they've gone."

While Rab darted off to return a moment later pushing a small barrow before him. "Look, Mairi, see what I've found. Father must have made it for me, must he not? I'll go and ask him."

Quickly Mairi stopped him. "No, Rab, not now! Why don't you give Archie a ride in the bonny cart?"

At this, Agnes screwed up her eyes and whined, "Me too, Rab, take me too."

Mairi's gentle voice soothed her, "Later, dear, Rab will take you later.

Now I'm going to make you a daisy-chain for your hair."

That night, when everyone had gone and Agnes and Archie Campbell were in possession of their new home, they looked at each other and smiled. With thick rugs covering the floor, polished chairs, table and stools in place, the glow of the fire lighting up the dusk, candles glimmering on the mantleshelf, it was all that a home should be.

The first thing Agnes Campbell had unpacked was

the Family Bible, which lay now on the table under her husband's hand.

The four children, washed and ready for bed, gathered round their parents and waited for their Bible story. Tonight, their Father read out the lovely words of the 23rd Psalm.

> The Lord is my Shepherd, I shall not want.
> He maketh me to lie down in green pastures;
> He leadeth me beside the still waters.
> He restoreth my soul;
> He leadeth me in the paths of righteousness
> for His name's sake:
> Yea, though I walk through the valley of the
>   shadow of death,
> I will fear no evil; for Thou art with me;
> Thy rod and Thy staff they comfort me.
> Thou preparest a table before me
> in the presence of mine enemies;
> Thou anointest my head with oil;
> my cup runneth over.
> Surely goodness and mercy shall follow me
>   all the days of my life, and I will dwell in
>   the house of the Lord for ever.

Mairi felt a stirring in her heart as she listened to her Father's voice and she whispered to herself, " . . . and I will dwell in the house of the Lord for ever."

As they bowed their heads in prayer and her Father asked the Lord to "bless this house and all who dwell therein" their murmured response was heartfelt.

Soon, it was the first day of school, and Agnes Campbell plaited Mairi's shining golden hair into a braid which she tied with a blue ribbon. Mairi smoothed down the cream apron which covered her dark blue dress and held up a foot to admire her new shoes of soft leather made for her by her Father.

Her Mother's voice caught her attention. "Mairi, look after Robert and see that he behaves himself," – this, as Rab squirmed under his Mother's hand in a vain attempt to escape her ministrations.

Agnes Campbell held him firmly by the shoulders, giving him a little shake to make him pay attention. "Now, Robert Campbell, you will listen to your sister, and it is myself that will see you right into the school yard."

Mairi's good nature was sorely tried as she held firmly to her brother's hand. Once he tore free to chase after a cat; a little later, he was off again to intervene with two snapping, snarling dogs, this to Mairi's great alarm. She warned him, "Behave, Rab, our Mother is seeing you from the window and it is herself will be at you when school is out."

The rebel glanced back, saw his Mother was indeed looking down the road and desisted from further forays. His lively mind casting ahead, he asked, "Mairi, what like is the teacher?"

"Father said he is a good man. He has the Gaelic and the English that we will have to learn and I fear that is a thing I cannot do."

Then Rab, who truly loved his sister, squeezed her hand and said, "Never mind, Mairi, I will help you. I can say some words already, words I learned from Andy the herd-boy at Bally Farm. He is a Lowlander, but that is not his fault." This last remark was said in a pitying tone of voice.

And so began Mairi's new life in Campbeltown, with days of school, of new friends, of helping her Mother; running errands, feeding the hens, ducks and geese;

paddling in the sea; climbing the hills to hear the wind sighing through the trees. Days so filled with happiness there never seemed enough time for all the little things. These were the joyous, fleeting days of her youth.

All too soon, Mairi had passed her fourteenth birthday, and had to leave her school days behind her. As was the custom, her parents arranged for her to go into Domestic Service, but because the House at Ballachontie was close to home, Mairi came back each night in the farm cart.

This tranquil life continued uninterrupted, until Mairi reached the age of sixteen and ended in an unexpected way. One Sunday, the Church had a Visiting Minister, the Reverend David Campbell from Loch Ranza in the Isle of Arran.

A distant cousin of Agnes Campbell, he had been invited to dine with them after the Service, with the express purpose of meeting their daughter, Mairi. Agnes and Archie Campbell had been surprised to hear that praise of Mairi's virtues had reached the ears of the Reverend David and his wife, in Arran, and he had planned his visit to see her for himself.

He told her parents that, if she pleased him, she would be offered a well-paid position in his household, to take charge of his two young children.

Unaware of his scrutiny, Mairi helped her Mother serve the meal; her pleasant manner, her gentleness with her brothers and sister, favourably impressed the Minister. "Aye," he thought, "she is all that they say about her, good-natured and kind-hearted, well able to help my wife with the children."

Agnes Campbell told Rab to take his brother and sister into the garden, bidding Mairi to stay behind as the Reverend David had something to say to her.

At first, Mairi listened to David Campbell in total incomprehension; words dropped into her mind . . . "you will like Loch Ranza, Mairi . . . a room of your own, next to the children . . . two little girls . . . you will see your Father when his boat calls at Arran . . . "

Suddenly she felt as if she had stepped into a basin of ice and the coldness of shock travelled from her feet all through her body and she gasped under it, a gasp she quickly stifled. Her blue eyes sought her Father's face, and her Mothers, and when she saw how anxiously they watched her, she forced a smile to her lips. She knew they would never insist that she went to Arran, but she sensed how disappointed they would be if she lost this fine opportunity.

Summoning all her courage, Mairi turned to the Minister and said, "I thank you, Reverend Campbell, for so kindly offering me the charge of your children. It is honoured I am to accept it, and happy I will be to go with you to Loch Ranza."

With these words, Mairi Campbell's childhood ended and her growing-up years began.

CHAPTER 5
Mary leaves Arran

Mairi Campbell cast a swift look round the little room which had been hers for the past two years. There, on that narrow bed, she had wept bitter tears of homesickness, as she had thought of her parents, her brothers and sister. On that first night, her usually sunny nature had deserted her and she had sobbed herself to sleep.

Now, on the point of departure, she smiled to think how quickly she had adjusted. Her two charges, aged three and one, were sweet-tempered, affectionate little things and the Reverend David and his wife had been kindness itself to her.

She turned to the window, which looked out onto a sandy beach and blue water sparkling in the sunshine. How many happy days had been spent there with the children, gathering little pink shells and red sea-urchins. She could see the Church, where the Reverend Campbell preached on the Sabbath, the familiar words from the Bible a comfort to her mind, whether they were gentle or sounded a stern warning of the dangers of straying from His teaching.

After church, many a hopeful swain would linger in the hope of winning some favour from the lovely, golden-haired girl, but the Minister shepherded her closely home and Mairi's unawareness of their ardent glances were her sure safeguard.

At the same moment that Mrs Campbell called to ask her if she was ready, Mairi caught sight of the rust-red sail of her Father's boat as it approached the bay.

Turning to go, Mairi was glad that Mrs Campbell had sent the children out with the new nursemaid, to spare them, she said, the sight of their beloved Mairi's departure.

The Reverend Campbell took charge of Mairi's belongings and together he and his wife accompanied her to the pier.

While they waited for her Father to tie-up his boat, David Campbell said, "We are truly sorry to be losing you, Mairi. You have been like a daughter to us." At which his wife whispered tearfully, "That is true, my dear. And I hope that our own little ones will grow up to emulate their much loved Mairi."

A steady stream of people began to arrive, all wanting to bid goodbye to the girl they had come to know and love.

Mairi was deeply touched as gifts were shyly handed to her – flowers in tight posies; a soft knitted shawl from a woman with gnarled fingers; a polished shell on which the old sailor had carved a ship in full sail; a necklace of Mother-of-pearl. The Scots dislike of showing emotion was forgotten as kisses were pressed on Mairi's cheek, so overwhelming her that she was glad of her Father's supporting arm as she boarded the boat that was taking her home. At this thought, Mairi waved once more to her friends on the pier, then turned to face towards Campbeltown, and home.

Agnes Campbell was waiting to greet her daughter, and drew her close in a loving embrace, and Mairi clung to her Mother as though she would never let her go.

This tender moment was interrupted by Rab, Agnes and Archie, all clamouring for Mairi's attention, their words pouring out like a burn in spate. Laughing, Mairi handed out the presents she had brought, a model ship for Rab, an embroidered collar for Agnes, a carved whistle for Archie. For her Mother there was a pink shell brooch and a goose-quill pen for her Father.

When the younger ones were in bed, Mairi sat down with her Mother and Father and waited for them to speak, to tell her why she had been brought back from Arran.

Agnes Campbell looked at her husband, who seemed to have some difficulty finding words. At last he said, "This has all been very sudden, Mairi, and truth to tell, we have had a hard time deciding what to do. You remember Miss Elizabeth Campbell, second cousin to your Mother? Well, she is Housekeeper to a lady in a grand Mansion in Ayrshire and has need of someone to serve in her house. She has asked Cousin Elizabeth if she could find such a one, and it is much to your credit that she at once thought of you."

Mairi stared at her Father, her thoughts in confusion, as she stammered, "You mean, I am to go away to Ayrshire, Father? To the Lowlands?"

Agnes Campbell leaned across to take her daughter's hands, saying softly, "It is not so very far, Mairi, and Elizabeth will look well after you. She tells us that you will have the company of young people, and will learn to speak the English with their help. Also, the wages are high, and a portion of them will be set aside for your Dowry. If, after a year, you are wishful to come home, that will be arranged. We have made this clear to Elizabeth and she has agreed."

Her Father added, "You will write to us, Mairi, and

tell us of life in the West country and I will write to you of all that happens here. Also, I will see you whenever the boat calls at Troon." Rising to his feet, he took something from the mantleshelf and put it in Mairi's hand. When she unwrapped the paper, she caught her breath in delight.

"Why, Father, two Bibles! So small they are." And, opening each in turn, she said, "One Bible is in the Gaelic, and one in the English?"

At her puzzled look, her Father smiled, "What better way to improve your English? You will read a passage each night in Gaelic, and read the same verses in the English. Will you be my good girl and do this for me?"

Mairi looked at him with love. "Yes, Father, I promise. And I thank you for my gift. When I read from them, it will remind me of home."

Miss Elizabeth Campbell arrived a week later to inspect Mairi before taking her to Ayrshire. Tall, spare of figure, dressed entirely in black, a beribboned bonnet framed a thin, long-nosed face. Sharp, pale blue eyes scanned the tall girl standing quietly before her, missing no detail of her appearance. She noted the golden hair neatly braided around her head, the deep blue eyes meeting her gaze respectfully, but not subservient. Elizabeth Campbell liked what she saw. She nodded to her cousin Agnes and, her tone brisk and kindly, said, "Your daughter looks to be a credit to you, Cousin. You need have no fear for her. She will be well looked after at Montgomerie House."

Turning to Mairi, she handed her a small packet, saying, "This tea is for your Mother, and perhaps you could prepare a cup for us while we discuss arrangements."

When Mairi went into the kitchen, Agnes Campbell

listened with close attention to all that her cousin had to say about life in the Ayrshire Mansion, with it's richly furnished rooms, great gardens, farms, dairies, and its servants. "Young things, most of them and mostly Lowlanders with none of the Gaelic. It will be good for Mairi to have companions of her own age and their conversation will help to improve her English, once she has got used to their Lowland accent."

As Mairi poured out the fragrant, pale gold tea and served the little honey and oatmeal cakes, Elizabeth Campbell noted the quiet economy of her movements. Again, she congratulated herself on her choice of Mairi to serve in Montgomerie House. Proud of her lineage, she looked forward to introducing Mairi to her friends, certain that she would be a credit to the name of Campbell.

CHAPTER 6

Montgomerie House

As the servants of Montgomerie House gathered round the long kitchen table, Mairi Campbell felt as if she were in a place of Bedlam. Barely able to distinguish faces and names, the language was beyond her comprehension as everyone spoke at once in a totally strange dialect. To Mairi, English was difficult enough, with its different sounds and structure, but this Lowland Scots was much, much worse. She doubted if she would ever be able to understand it.

She heard her name called, not the soft Gaelic, "Mairi" but a sharper sound, the Scots name of "Mary". She looked to see who had spoken and recognised the Cook, one Jessie Smith, a big, sonsy young woman in spotless white apron and cap. She beckoned, saying, "Come and sit here, Mary. I want to talk to you." This was said in plain English, to Mairi's great relief. Here was someone she could understand well enough to follow what was said.

Eyes followed the slim golden-haired girl as she moved gracefully to the head of the table. When she had arrived a week ago, she had caused quite a stir when it was known that the dignified Housekeeper, Miss Campbell, had her under her special care. When the Cook, the undisputed ruler of the kitchen, took Mary under her wing, she ensured there would be no bullying, had her fellow-workers been so inclined. They still giggled at Mary's quaint way of pronouncing her words, but there was no malice behind it and Mary, in any case, seemed not to notice.

Jessie Smith ladled rich soup into Mary's bowl, telling her briskly to help herself to bread from the wooden platter. She noted Mary's glance moving from one to another of the servants and smiled to herself. She guessed that the girl was putting a name to each one; brown-haired Betty Morrison, her fellow Dairymaid and room mate; under-cook Jean Purdie, fiery redhead; scullery maid Effie, skinny and tough; bald Willie, the odd-job man and squint-eyed Jimmy, gardener's boy. Later there would be another sitting for the Coachmen, the Stablemen and the Gardeners, who preferred to eat without the "clacking" of the women.

There was silence now around the table as every-one paid serious attention to their food, which at Montgomerie House was never stinted, and Jessie Smith was an excellent cook.

Mary glanced shyly at Jessie, thinking how handsome she was, with glossy black hair, red cheeks and dark eyes. She blushed when she realised that Jessie was returning her look with interest, laughing as she did so, asking now, "Well, Mary Campbell, and what is your opinion of us all? For I'll warrant you have one, stored away in that head of yours."

Mary did not reply, being unable to put her thoughts into words. She could not express her feeling of compassion when she watched Effie struggle with loads too heavy for her thin body and, whenever she could, relieved the girl of her burden. She did not know this was the first kindness Effie had ever known.

Jessie Smith now said, "Mary, I like the way you

make the butter and the cheese, and Mistress Mont-gomerie has remarked that they have much improved." Raising her voice, she spoke across the table to Betty Morrison, "I told the Mistress, Betty, that it is you we have to thank for putting Mary in charge of the Buttery."

Betty, a happy-natured young woman, smiled and nodded. "Aye? That was kind of you, Cook, to say so, but truth to tell, I was doing myself a good turn. It's real hard work, churning butter, and I don't have the knack of it. Milking is more in my line, and thanks to Mary, I've got more time for it."

The gardener's boy, Jimmy, looked over at Mary. She had won his heart by never once remarking on his squint, not even seeming to notice it. Mary felt his gaze on her and smiled, a dimple appearing beside her soft mouth.

Jimmy blushed, and in his confusion said the first thing that came into his head. "Is it true that your Father's Captain o' a boat, Mary?"

Struggling to understand his words, her answer came slowly. "My Father, yess, of a boat he iss the Captain."

"If he's a Captain, how is it you're working here as dairymaid?" Jean's broad accent and her quick speech, defeated Mary, who looked to the Cook for help.

Jessie spoke tartly. "And what is wrong with being a dairymaid? Our Miss Campbell is related to Mary's family, and it was she who brought her here. Now stop your clackin' and finish your meal. Tomorrow is Saturday and we've all the cooking and cleaning to do before the Sabbath. As well, it will soon be time for the men, so get on with you."

In their room that night, Betty undressed to her shift and jumped under the blankets. She watched as Mary, stripped to a cotton bodice, washed herself with cold water, unbound her hair and braided it into one long 'pigtail' to hang down her back, before slipping on her nightdress. Sitting on the edge of her bed, she opened one of her Bibles and read it silently, her lips moving as her eyes followed the words. Betty knew that Mary was reading her Gaelic Bible and, curious, she asked her, "Why have you got two Bibles, Mary? Isn't one enough?"

Mary looked up. "My Father gave me the two of them before I left home and I promised to read a verse each night, first in the Gaelic, and then in the English. I am not very good in the English, see you." Betty had a sudden inspiration. "I know! I will read the English verses aloud for you and that will help with your saying of it. I learned to read at the Sunday School, from the Bible. Show me what you are reading." Mary handed over her English version, opened at Proverbs, chapter 30 and pointed to verses 18 and 19.

Slowly, painstakingly, Betty read the words.

> There be three things which are too
>   wonderful for me,
> yea, four which I know not:
> the way of an eagle in the air;
> the way of a serpent upon a rock;
> the way of a ship in the midst of the sea;
> and the way of a man with a maid.

Wide-eyed, Betty said, "Why, Mary, these are pictures of things I know well. I've seen eagles, high up in the sky, and, well, maybe not a serpent on a rock, but wee grass snakes in the sun and of course you know all about ships at sea and . . . " here she broke off with a blush, "the way of a man with a maid. Well, that's my Davie with his sweet-talk when we walk out together. But now it's your turn to read." She listened as Mary read, slowly, stumblingly, but correctly, her soft Highland voice making music of the words.

After kneeling to say her prayers, Mary composed herself to sleep. She thought of eagles and serpents, of her Father's ship sailing into the bay, but of a man with a maid she could make no picture. Drowsiness drifted into sleep, and silence fell in the little room.

The next evening, all the cleaning and polishing was done in the big, square kitchen; wood and coal filled the scuttles; brasses shone like gold; food was piled on serving dishes and covered with snowy white cloths. Supper had been served and cleared away and now the exhausted servants were able to relax.

The girls talked of their sweethearts, of walking with them to Church and of having their company in the kitchen afterwards. Peppery, red-haired Jean was "walking-out" with the elderly head gardener, a widower with no family; Betty had her Davie, the young coachman and Effie had hopes of capturing Jimmy's attention, though so far she had been unsuccessful.

Presently the talk became more general as they speculated who would be at the Church from the village and neighbouring farms. Jean Purdie, green eyes glinting, said, "I hear that Robert Burns is back at Mossgiel, and if that is so, maybe we'll see him in the Kirk the morn."

The others were variously affected by this piece of news, Jessie Smith disapproving, Betty excited and Effie all agape for a glimpse of the young Farmer.

The Cook snapped at her. "A wee look at him, say you! If that lad turns up, its little attention the Minister will get from a' the silly lassies.

"Och, Jessie, ye cannae blame the lassies for wanting a look at him, for ye cannot deny he's the handsomest lad in the parish. If I hadna' got my Davie, I'd angle for him myself!

"Betty Morrison, it's soft in the heid ye are, and I wonder at ye. Think shame to be so brazen! If you "angled" after Master Burns, like as not you'd find yourself a seat on the Sinner's Stool. You forget such daftness and hold fast to your Davie, aye, and think yourself lucky to have him!"

Not a whit daunted, Betty tossed her head and declared, "Aye, maybe so, but Davie canna' write braw poetry like Robert Burns." This so angered Jessie that she rose to her feet in wrath and ordered them all to bed. Mary had not paid much heed to the dispute, much of which she had not understood, but the name "Robert" had reminded her of her brother Rab, and she smiled to think of him as a writer of poems, and smilingly, imagined his disgust at the very idea.

CHAPTER 7

Burns first sees
Highland Mary

In the farm of Mossgiel, Robert Burns presented himself for his Mother's inspection, a ritual begun in boyhood before setting out for Church.

Agnes Burns looked at her eldest son, the head of the family since his Father's death five months ago, and swept her gaze over him from head to foot and back again. Tall, broad-shouldered, his cut-away coat of good maroon cloth fitted him well, and the white stock emphasised the square, cleft chin. His black hair swept down his face in neat side-burns and as she met his gaze, his brown eyes smiled down at her with affection.

"Well, Mother, will I do?" he asked, with laughter in his voice.

Mrs Burns nodded once. "Aye, Robert, you'll do." These words were, for her, high praise. "You're early for the Kirk, but I suppose you'll be calling in for John Lees. Give his Mother my greetings." Then, unable to stop herself, she said, "Your Father would be proud to see you, laddie, that he would."

Robert's black brows drew together, and there was a brooding heaviness in his voice as he answered, "I'm not sure of that, Mother. You know he never really forgave me for taking Gilbert to the Dancing. He blamed me for leading him into ungodly habits."

His Mother shook her head in denial, and to take the pain from her eyes, he lightened his look and spoke gently. "It's all right, Mother. I didn't mean that. None could have had a better Father, and I wish he could have been spared to us. But now it's time for me to go, else I'll be late for the Sermon."

Robert's words almost came true, and the doors of the Church were about to close as he and John Lees squeezed through, to the muttered imprecations of the Beadle.

Heads craned round to see the cause of the commotion and as Burns settled on his seat his quick eye took note of the one head that had not turned.

If Mary Campbell had planned to attract the young man's attention she could not have devised a surer way. But no such thought was in her mind. Eyes closed, head bowed, she was deep in prayer, lost to everything and everyone around her.

Robert Burns paid less heed than usual to the Minister until he thundered forth from the Book of Job.

"There was a man in the land of Uz, whose name was Job, and that man was perfect and upright and one that feared God and eschewed evil." These words were the basis of his sermon and Burns eyes hardened as the Reverend Aulds stared directly at him from the Pulpit.

John Lees nudged him and whispered, "Man, Robbie, we're in for it now! Daddy Auld must have been listening to gossip. No' very Christian of the Minister, would ye say?"

"Christian? That hypocrite! None of his servant lassies are safe from him. And it's not you he's getting at, John. It's me. He cannot abide my writing, especially when I get at the Kirk." Then he dismissed the Minister from his mind. "Enough of him! Tell me, John, who is the lass sitting two rows down on the right? Wearing a grey dress with a white collar and a white bonnet?"

John Lees looked and shook his head. "I can't see her face, Robert, but she's with the servants from Montgomerie House. I did hear tell of a new dairymaid they call 'Mary from the Highlands'. Maybe that's the lassie." Then he squinted sideways at his friend, noting the intensity of his interest as he gazed raptly at the unknown girl, and was moved to ask, "Robert, what's come over you that you're so taken with a lass whose face you've never seen? Suppose she turns out to be as ugly as poor Beenie Scott, with her squashed nose and pockie face?" At this, Burns shook his head and made no answer. John would see soon enough how wrong he was.

The service ended with the Benediction, and the congregation filed slowly out into the sunlight, to stand around in groups, talking to their friends.

The servant girls from Montgomerie, walking in pairs, bobbed curtsies to John Lees while casting their eyes at his companion.

Burns bowed slightly and smiled as he acknowledged the coy glances of Betty and Effie, but all his attention was focused on the slender girl who accompanied Jessie Smith. He was aware of Jessie saying, "Good morning, Mr Lees, Mr Burns." And he heard himself reply, without taking his gaze from Mary as he willed her to look at him. For one brief moment she lifted her head and their eyes met, deep blue to dark brown, and then, blushing furiously she was gone.

Burns was left with an impression of golden hair, an oval face, and eyes so deeply blue they reminded him of speedwells. In a daze, he was recalled to his senses by

John Lees' drawn-out whistle, hastily suppressed by disapproving tuts from bystanders.

"Aye, Robert, you were quite right! What a beauty! But how you could see that from the back only is beyond me." He clapped his friend on the back and joked, "If you hadn't seen the lass first, I would have cast my cap at her myself."

Burns turned and gave Lees a look, such a one as to make him step back, saying hastily, "'Tis only joking I am, Robert. Only joking!" adding to himself, "and pity help me if I was not!"

Jessie Smith had witnessed Burns' interest in Mary, had seen the look they had exchanged and had been startled by Mary's blushing reaction. As they walked arm-in-arm along the tree-lined path, she wondered what to do for the best. Should she warn Mary about Burns? That would mean telling her about his reputation as a womaniser, his love-them-and-leave-them philosophy.

In fairness, Jessie admitted to herself, this was only one side of the coin; on the other side, he was a good son to his Mother, worked hard on his farm and was considered a poet of no small merit. Handsome enough to steal any girl's heart, but not exactly the Godly man of the sermon! Jessie's thoughts had come full circle and left her still perplexed. Maybe she had read more into the incident that it warranted and no more would come of it. Jessie's commonsense nature came to her rescue and she decided to think no more about it.

Mary, unusually silent, was lost in her own thoughts. She remembered a handsome face, with glowing brown eyes that held her own, sending a message she could not understand but which sent the hot colour to her cheeks as she recalled it.

Robert Burns and John Lees took the path round

by Failford, with Burns in a deeply thoughtful mood. "John," he asked, "have you not anyone you know working in Montgomerie?"

John Lees, shoemaker and blackfoot, that is to say, a 'matchmaker', was known in many of the big houses around Mauchline, but at his friend's question, he shook his head. "No, Robert, I've never been inside the place. Och, I know the lassies and I am acquainted with the Cook, but that's about the size of it."

Burns groaned aloud. "John, John, you'll have to do better than that. I must meet the lass, and soon, and I cannot do it without your help."

Lees had never known Burns so wrought up over any lass, and, willing to help, he said, "Well, see you, Rob, there's a wee chink o' hope. I know the young coachman who's walking out with one of the dairymaids. Maybe I'll have a word with him, see if he'll wangle me an introduction to the Cook. I'll let on I have a fancy for her and that might get me into the House."

At this, Burns gripped his friend's arm, saying, "John, you must waste no time! Go and see the lad tomorrow and bring me word to the East field. If you do this for me, I'll give you my best silver buckles."

Rubbing his arm vigorously where Burns had gripped it, Lees said aggrievedly, "Losh sakes, Robert, I think you've paralysed my arm! What's come over you? You've never lacked sweethearts and never cared a docken which one came running. What's made you so fierce for this one?"

But he got no answer save a shake of the head as Burns strode off towards Mossgiel.

John Lees set out the next morning to find his friend Davie in the coachyard. "Good day to you Davie," he called, which greeting caused Davie's head to withdraw with a bump from the interior of the coach, a duster in his hand. "John, what brings you out so early in the day?" he exclaimed in astonishment.

Drawing close, Lees wasted no time in disclosing his errand "Well, Davie, it's this way. I want your help in arranging a meeting for me at the Big House. On behalf of a friend you might say."

Davie stared at Lees and with more than a hint of suspicion he asked, "And who might your friend be, and what lassie would you be spiering after?"

John laughed and patted Davie's shoulder. "Now, now Davie, don't be so danged quick with your guessing! My friend you ken well enough, he's Robert Burns of Mossgiel, and truth to tell, I dinnae ken the lass's name, but she was at the Kirk yesterday. Tall, fair hair, right bonny."

"That will be Mary Campbell, the new dairymaid with my lass Betty. But Mossgiel will find no easy conquest there."

"How so? She's a lass, isn't she? And Rob knows well how to woo the lasses with his bonny poetry and his braw words."

Davie laughed. "That's just it, Johnny, the lass won't understand any of his fine words or his poetry! She is from the Highlands and speaks the Gaelic or the pure English. Our Scots speech she grasps only with difficulty, so I'm told. But she is well-liked and everyone tries to help her."

John Lees was nonplussed, wondering how Burns would react to a lass who spoke and thought in another language. Then he shrugged, telling himself that all he had to do was arrange the meeting; after that, it was for Fate and Robert to decide.

Burns was in the East field, repairing the drystone

dyke, turning every few minutes to search the road for a sight of John Lees. Mechanically, he went on lifting the heavy stones into place, wondering what was keeping Lees and how much longer he would have to wait. So deep was he in his thoughts he failed to hear his name being called and not until John, fingers in mouth, let out a piercing whistle did he drop the stone he was holding and swing around.

His friend, jacket slung over his shoulder, cried cheerfully, "Is it deaf you are, Rob? I was certain sure I'd find you glowerin' over the dyke like a lovesick calf and here you are, not a bit bothered to hear my news! Ah well, I'll just away back the way I came. Guid day to you." He pretended to walk off and Burns, infuriated by his teasing, leapt over the wall and grabbed him.

"John, I swear if you don't stop your nonsense and give me your news, I'll forget we are friends and do you an injury."

Soothingly, but swiftly, Lees got his word in. "It's good news, Robert, good news! If you will just unhand me, maybe I could sit down and get my wind back. It is a long, thirsty walk I've had and here is fine thanks ye give me."

With his first words Burns's passion faded. He picked up his friend and with one easy movement had him over the wall. Dropping down beside him, he handed him a jug of ale and waited till he had quenched his thirst.

"Ah, Rob, I needed that! Well, the lass is called Mary, Mary Campbell and I'm to meet the Cook on Wednesday at Montgomerie, to arrange for you to call on her."

Softly, Burns repeated her name, "Mary Campbell." John quickly told him the rest. "There's something you have to know, Robert. The lass is only able to understand a wee bit of the English, and not much at all of our Lowland tongue. Will that not be a hindrance to you?"

Burns threw back his head and laughed. "A hindrance? never! For her I will put aside the Doric and speak to her only in the English she will understand."

When it was known that John Lees was to call at Montgomerie to arrange a meeting between Robert Burns and Mary Campbell, it called forth an outburst of amazement. Betty and Effie were openly envious, but Jean Purdie could not hide her spiteful malice. Green eyes glinting with fury, she vented her spleen on Mary.

"So, the young poet, Mossgiel has taken a fancy to our Highland Mary! Oh, I saw the way he looked at you outside the Church, but wait till he finds out you can't speak a word of his language." She broke off to laugh shrilly. "But then, it's not likely to be words he's after, is it?"

At this, seeing Mary's confusion, Jessie Smith rounded on her tormentor. "You hold your tongue, you bad-minded besom, and leave Mary alone. You'd like it to be you that Robert Burns was coming for, wouldn't you? But all you'll ever get will be your old gardener, and lucky to get him at that, for nobody else would have you!"

Jean Purdie, speechless with fury, made no reply. She couldn't afford to antagonise the Cook, as she knew well it might cost her the job, which she badly needed.

Jean Purdie's attack on Mary helped Jessie to make up her mind, and when John Lees asked for an appointment for Burns to call, Jessie's consent was given for the next Sunday evening. As well as this, she had agreed that he might walk with Mary after the Church service, while Lees would follow with herself as chaperone.

CHAPTER 8

A Meeting is
Arranged

On the morning that he was to meet Mary Campbell, Robert Burns was too late for the Kirk. Just as he was setting off, his brother Gilbert came to him with a badly gashed hand, and Robert turned back to attend to him. When he was done, he snatched up his hat and rushed out, knowing he could never make it before the doors closed.

Half-way there, he met John Lees coming to see what kept him. Burns explained what had happened, ending with a sigh, "I wish it hadn't happened on this day of all days."

Nothing loath to miss a long-winded sermon, Lees was not at all put out. "Well Rabbie, we were not to meet the lassie till she comes out of the Kirk, so we'll just daunder at our leisure. When she sees you waiting for her, she'll think you were inside the whole time."

But John Lees was wrong. Mary Campbell sensed that Burns was not in the Church. For the first time, she found it difficult to concentrate on the Service. Only during Prayers was she able to find comfort in the well-known words, which calmed her unrest. Later, doubts crept in to torment her; had the blackfoot's visit been a joke? And was his friend a party to it? The thought made her blush for shame and she dreaded to think of the remarks of Jean Purdie and her cruel laughter. More than shame, she felt hurt and strangely disappointed until she remembered brown eyes looking deep into her own, and she was comforted.

As they walked out into the sunlight, Jessie Smith tucked her hand through Mary's arm. She too had taken note that neither John Lees nor Robert Burns were present and she vowed if they didn't turn up, Lees would get a flyting that would scorch his ears for many a day.

Almost immediately, Jessie and Mary spotted the two young men waiting for them in the same place as the Sunday before. Involuntarily, Jessie tightened her grip on Mary's arm as she felt it quiver under her grasp. John Lees stepped forward, bowed first to Jessie, then to Mary, saying respectfully, "Mistress Smith, Mistress Campbell, may I present my friend, Mr Robert Burns of Mossgiel."

With that, Burns stepped forward and made his bow, careful to address Jessie first before turning his gaze on Mary.

In response to his greeting, Jessie said, "Mr Burns," and gave him a slight nod in acknowledgement, while Mary dipped in a slight graceful curtsey, but said no word. Aware of the audible comments of the other servants, she felt herself blush even more deeply.

Jessie turned, and fixing the chatterers with a no-nonsense glare, motioned them on ahead. She beckoned John Lees to her side and allowed Burns and Mary to walk behind them, a rare concession on her part to Mary's shy modesty.

Although her eyes were lowered and they walked well apart from one another, Mary was acutely conscious of her companion's presence, as he was of hers.

Burns could not keep his eyes from Mary as he noted

everything about her; her tall, graceful figure; the way the long, curling lashes, rested on her cheeks, a darker gold than her hair; the way the soft, red lips turned up, as if ready to smile; a sweetly rounded, dimpled chin.

Suddenly he wanted to see her smile, hear her voice. With a swift gesture he stopped to pick a cluster of tiny flowers. Mary, startled, waited for him to resume his place by her side and curiosity made her look to see what had caused him to stop so abruptly. The darkly handsome face she so well remembered, broke into a smile and with a bow he held out to her the flowers he had picked, saying in a deep, warm voice, "For you, Miss Campbell. Speedwells, as blue as your eyes."

Blushing, Mary accepted the flowers, saying, "It is thanking you I am, Mr Burns, for your kind words, and pleased I am to hear you speak the English. The other tongue, the Scots? I find hard on my ears."

"It is hard to understand, and I have my old teacher to thank for my skill with the English. But is not Gaelic your Mother tongue?" Puzzling this out, Mary replied slowly, "Indeed yes, for me the first, the best, is the Gaelic. Some English I learned, I fear not well, in Campbeltown. Now I am in Montgomerie and another tongue must I learn, much stranger to me than the English."

There was no self-pity in her voice, only a matter-of-fact acceptance of her lot, but Burns felt his heart go out to her. He wondered how she must feel, living in a community where, every day, she was surrounded by a people totally alien to her. Compassion swept him, and with it a fierce urge to protect and help her in every way he could.

After seeing Mary and Jessie into the House, with the prospect of calling on them that evening, Burns and Lees set off on the path through Montgomerie Woods.

Lees, anxious to know how his friend had fared with Mary, plied him with eager questions.

"Well, Robert, did you find the lass to your liking? Were you able to talk with her or is it true what they say, that she's just Highland Mary, with no speech in our tongue?"

Burns turned on him in anger. "*Just* Highland Mary, and no words in our tongue? It ill becomes you, John Lees, to repeat such gossip! Tell me, how many words of Gaelic do you know? And have those others ever learned to speak the King's English? Well, while you're scratching your head over that think on this, Mary speaks the English better that those villifiers ever will, as well as the Gaelic and now she has set herself to learn our Lowland Scots, which will make three languages. Suppose, just suppose, that you found yourself in a place where only the Gaelic was spoken, or French or Greek? How would you feel? Not a soul to talk with you, only sideways looks and names whispered behind hands. No, you would not like it and you wouldn't behave half as well as Mary Campbell!"

Lees, with absolutely nothing to say in answer to Robert's attack, wisely kept quiet as he continued. "As to finding the lass to my liking, I only hope she will look on me with equal favour."

Used as he was to his friend's mercurial temperament, John Lees reflected that this was Burns in a mood unlike any he had seen before. What would become of this new relationship he could not even hazard a guess. Whistling soundlessly through pursed lips, he thought, only time will tell.

Jessie Smith readily agreed to Mary's suggestion of a walk, as did Robert Burns and John Lees when they presented themselves at seven o'clock.

The summer evening was warm, with the hot blue

sky of daytime cooled to soft pink and gold. Mary led them through the fields to her favourite retreat, a white hawthorn tree, heavy with the scented, flowering clusters that provided a drooping shade beneath it's branches. Through the trailing fronds could be seen a wooden seat, encircling the gnarled tree-trunk, bathed in the reflected light of the green leaves. His imagination stirred by this sight, Burns exclaimed, "Why, Mary, it is an enchanted cave you have found, under green water!" and, holding out his hand to her said, "Come, let us go in."

Having seated Mary, Burns turned to Jessie, who hastily refused to enter, saying she had no wish to have "beasties" dropping onto her head. Instead, she chose to walk beside the stream with Lees, leaving Mary and Burns to share a few moments of privacy beneath the hawthorn's flowering screen.

The sun, filtering through the branches, turned Mary's hair into a shining nimbus. Burns gazed at it in fascination saying, "Your hair, Mary, is purest gold, a gold of many colours. I see red, yellow and a shade the colour of beech leaves in Autumn. You should never cover it up!"

Unable to meet his admiring glance, Mary looked down at her hands and made no answer, but was glad he found her pleasing. She did not guess that he longed to release the braided coronet from its pins, allowing her hair to fall, untramelled, to her waist. Wise enough to practise restraint, he merely touched his finger to one loose curl on her cheek and caught his breath as he imagined how it would feel to bury his face in the whole, glowing mass. So strongly did he desire it that he had to exert all of his strong will to banish it from his mind. He began to talk in a friendly way of everyday things and soon Mary's confusion was forgotten as she listened to what he was saying, "You have not been here very long, Mary, but maybe you have heard about the 'Holy Fair'?"

"Yes, this I have heard, but understand I do not. How can a thing be 'Holy' and also be a Fair? Is not 'Holy' for the things of the Church?"

The lilt of her voice, the soft sibilance of her words, so captivated Burns that he forgot all about the 'Holy Fair' and instead asked, "Mary would you, for me, say 'Robert' in your own language?"

Although surprised at this unexpected request, Mary did as he asked and from her soft lips, his Gaelic name of 'Raibeart' fell sweetly on his ears. Gently, he reached out to touch her hand, saying simply, sincerely, "Thank you, Mary. You have made my name a thing most pleasing to hear."

Straightening his back against the trunk of the tree, he began to tell her about the 'Holy Fair'. "It is held in August, on the Sabbath before the Communion, that will be in two weeks time. There will be a great visitation of Ministers, each one roaring louder than the other, to attract the biggest audience. That is the 'Holy' bit! But see you, not all their ranting can spoil the fun, when lads and lasses, the old folk and the bairns, set out to enjoy themselves. Will you come with me, Mary? Oh, I know I cannot have you all to myself, not when Jessie and the others are there, but will you be my partner?"

With a turn of her head, Mary saw that Jessie and John Lees were starting to walk back to them, and as she looked into the brown eyes that pleaded for her answer, she swiftly gave it, "Yes, Robert, I will come with you." Burns also had noted the imminent arrival of the others and, under his breath, condemned them silently to perdition. Reaching up, he plucked a sweet-scented spray of hawthorn blossom and, touching it to his lips, gave it to Mary with the words, "To remind you of our first tryst beneath your hawthorn tree."

That night, before going to bed, Mary learned more about the 'Holy Fair'. As a special treat, it being the Sabbath, Jessie had brewed a pot of her best tea, and poured for each one a generous cupful, served with honey and raisin cakes that melted in the mouth.

Drinking her tea with relish, she told Mary, "The morning of the Fair, the lads call here bright and early, to pick us up. We provide baskets of food and drink and they bring stools to sit on inside the tents, as well as horses and carts to get us to the big field." Here she was interrupted by Effie, who couldn't sit still for excitement.

"And just wait till you see the dancing bears and the dogs that jump through hoops and Tumblers and Jugglers and Gypsies and oh! wait till you see the stalls full of Fairings."

Betty explained, "That means trinkets, which your lad will buy you as a reminder of the Fair."

Jessie, in mellow mood, laughed, "Aye, and if you're not careful, a reminder of more than that!"

Mary, head spinning, had not understood one half of all they said, but thought it must be a very exciting event to arouse so much talk and laughter. For her, the pleasure was looking forward to a whole day in the company of Robert Burns, of seeing all the wonderful sights through his eyes, and Mary blushed at the thought, of reading in those eyes a message that he found her surpassing fair.

Saying her prayers that night, Mary Campbell added a new name to those for whom she asked a blessing, the name of Robert Burns.

CHAPTER 9
The Holy Fair

Feelings ran high in Montgomerie House on the morning of the 'Holy Fair' as everyone rushed to get ready. Effie giggled so hard she dropped a pile of plates and had her ears soundly boxed by the exasperated Cook, which effectively changed the giggles to loud and tearful howls. Jimmy tripped over the dog which fled, yelping, from his kicks and curses, while Jean Purdie and Betty Morrison wrangled noisily over baskets which each claimed as her own.

Mary, amidst all the noise and confusion, remained calm. She wiped Effie's tears and stopped her wails with a piece of cake, set out the oatmeal bannocks with thick wedges of cheese, and jugs of ale and milk, then quietly called on the others to sit down and eat. Worn out with all their strife, they were glad to rest their legs and their voices and peace fell over the table.

Mary sighed with relief as she savoured the silence and let her thoughts dwell on the happiness to come. Jessie had to jog her elbow to bring her out of her daydreams, saying sharply, "Mary, stop your wool gathering and help me clear away the dishes. It's after seven o'clock and we're nowhere near ready."

Springing to her feet, Mary passed plates and cups to the end of the table where Effie and Jimmy stacked them in the stone sinks, ready to be washed.

Betty had been keeping an anxious eye on the weather and now sought reassurance from the Cook. "It's awful dark, Jessie. Do you think it'll rain? Or worse, will it be thunder and lightning?"

This last brought a howl from Effie, who wailed piteously, "Och, I wish you hadnae said that, Betty. I'm that feared o' storms! Thunder's bad enough, but lightnin' might strike us a' stone deid!"

Jessie sharply nipped Effie's hysteria in the bud. "If you don't stop your nonsense my girl, I might just be tempted to strike you stone dead myself!" Then, switching her attack, she rounded on Betty, "See what your daftness has done, Betty Morrison! But maybe you're thinking to set yourself up as a weather prophet? Well, listen to this, it is to be a fine day, according to Jean's auld Willie. Isn't that so, Jean?"

Half angered at reference to her 'auld Willie', half pleased at being deferred to by Jessie, Jean tossed her red head and made tart reply. "No so much of the auld, Jessie Smith, but aye, he did say that. Mind you, he didnae rule out a wee shower or two."

Jessie dismissed this as not worth bothering about. "Sure, a droppie of rain never harmed anybody, but just in case, we'll take the canvas to put over us and there's always tents and sheds set up in the field for shelter." Work done, Mary and Betty hurried to their room to put the finishing touches to their costumes. Stripping off her apron, Betty revealed a flowered print dress, to the shoulders of which she attached knots of bright red and yellow ribbons.

Mary's dress was a simply cut blue cotton with no adornment save a white muslin fichu at the neck.

"Haven't you any ribbons, Mary? You look awful plain!"

Mary hid a smile at the hint of disapproval in Betty's voice. "Och yes, indeed I do, but only one ribbon I wish, for my hair, see you." When she had finished twining the deep blue ribbon into her golden coronet of braids, Betty had to admit that she "looked a treat" and wondered if she should tone down her own gaudy silk streamers.

The sound of horses' hooves, cartwheels and laughing male voices, caused the girls to snatch up handkerchiefs and purses before hurrying down to the kitchen. There, milling about in fine disarray, were the men – Jimmy, Davie the Coach, Willie the Gardener, John Lees and Robert Burns.

Burns thought he had never seen anyone so fresh and lovely as Mary. Her simple blue dress with snowy white kerchief, the blue ribbon in her golden hair, pleased him as no amount of frills and furbelows ever could.

Mary, on her part, noted how well Robert looked, his manly figure set off to advantage by his brown velveteen coat, brocade waistcoat and high-necked cravat, with fawn breeches tucked into leather topboots. Their eyes met, and happiness sparked between them, causing Mary to smile involuntarily while Burns laughed aloud in an exhilaration of high spirits.

John Lees broke into their moment, bowing to Mary and urging Burns to get a move on as everyone was waiting for them. Robert grabbed Mary's hand, snatched up one remaining basket, and swept her with him to join the others.

A resounding cheer came from the waiting carts when Mary and Robert appeared, bringing hot colour to Mary's cheeks. While Burns lifted her to sit beside him on the driver's seat, John Lees nimbly clambered up to join Jessie and sat as close to her ample figure as the stool allowed. For once, he was not rebuffed.

The Love of Highland Mary

Taking up the reins, Burns shook them so that the bells jingled and the horse broke into a trot, and the other carts fell in behind them. Mary looked with amazement at the crowds on the road, some on horseback, most on foot, carrying baskets and stools of all description. There was loud chatter, laughter and singing, with good-natured waves and greetings to the passing carts. Mary responded by waving her handkerchief and Robert flourished his beribboned whip, calling to those he knew by name.

As the cartwheels bounced over the ruts, it gave Burns the opportunity to slip his arm round Mary's slender waist to steady her and, glad of his support, she relaxed against him.

When they arrived, the great open space reserved for the Fair was so crowded it seemed impossible to find a place where they could leave their horse and cart. But at last it was done, with Lees exclaiming in disbelief, "Man, Robbie, do you see the prices? Water, one penny a bucket, oats, three pennies! It's highway robbery, that's what it is!"

"What else do you expect? It's always the same at the Fair. But there now, isn't it worth a few bawbees to see folk enjoying themselves?"

Then turning to Mary, Burns pointed to a group of Tumblers. "See there, Mary, would you like to take a look at them when we've seen to the horse?" Mary, blue eyes wide as she watched the swift somersaults of men clad in scarlet and yellow, was speechless, but her smile and the turn of her head, told Burns all he needed to know.

Business settled, the men removed the stools from the cart, and handed the baskets to Jessie and Mary. Taking Mary on his free arm, Burns led the way to the crowd gathered around the Tumblers, where, by vigorous nudging and use of elbows, he and John cleared a path to the edge of the display.

Boys and men, in brilliant tunics and tights, were now forming a pyramid by running and leaping onto one another's shoulders, ending with the smallest boy as the apex. To the loud applause of the crowd, they jumped down so swiftly the eye could not follow them and in a trice were darting round with caps for donations. Delighted to see Mary and Jessie transfixed with wonder, Burns and Lees gave generously and the young performer, as a 'thank you' placed his cap on the ground and did a hand-stand over it.

As they moved towards the largest tent, at every two steps they were accosted by sellers of food and favours. Robert, with his customary open-handedness, would have bought the lot, if Mary's slight shake of the head hadn't stopped him.

However, when a small girl in a ragged kirtle tugged his sleeve and begged, "Buy my apples, sir, for the bonny lady. Big and sweet and juicy they are. No worms inside," Mary's heart was melted. Burns selected four of the rosy fruits, overpaid by tuppence, and dropped them into Mary's basket.

On their other side, an old woman badgered John into buying a handful of sugar plums, but was not allowed by Jessie to pay more than half the pennies asked for them.

They reached the tent where Burns, from past experience, chose a space nearest to the turned back flap, which would be cool against the heat and a shelter if it rained. John Lees helped him place the stools, and Jessie and Mary pushed their baskets underneath.

A sudden, stentorian shout from the front caused heads to turn. "Robert! Robert Burns! Over here, man!"

Burns recognised the voice of his friend, Gavin Hamilton, and assessed the situation. He did not want to leave Mary, but felt that he could not ignore Hamilton's urgent invitation. He spoke to the others, while looking only at Mary. "I have to go over and have a word with my friend, Mr Hamilton. I won't be long. "John," turning to Lees, "look after the lassies till I get back."

They watched his tall figure stepping carefully over outstretched legs and looked with interest at Gavin Hamilton. They saw a thick-set man with a genial red face and receding, light brown hair, whose gold watch-chain was pulled tight over a rounded stomach.

Jessie, black eyes glinting with curiosity, remarked, "So, that is the Laird of Hamilton House, is it? He appears to be on right friendly terms with Robert."

John Lees answered airily, "Och, as to that, Robert met Mr Hamilton some years ago when we were at Tarbolton Masonic. He is a great admirer of Robert's poems and he's the one who leased Mossgiel to Rob and his brother Gilbert." He did not add that Gavin Hamilton was also a companion in many of their drinking and womanising escapades.

Jessie was restless as they waited for Burns to return. She was hungry and thirsy and desired to assuage these pangs before the arrival of the first preacher, and now said, "Mary, look and see if Robert is sitting down with Mr Hamilton's party, for if he is, I mean to open our baskets right away." Mary did as Jessie asked, for truth to tell, she too was hungry but knew that she would not enjoy the food if Robert were not there to share it with her. To her relief, she saw Robert stand up, as thought taking his leave of the Laird who, turning to glance in their direction, made them a deep courtly bow. Jessie and Mary dipped their heads in acknowledgement, Mary blushing at the unexpected compliment while John Lees saluted, a broad smile on his face.

It was as well that Mary had not heard the remarks that preceded Gavin Hamilton's gesture when, catching sight of her, he had whistled softly in appreciation, saying, "Well, Robert, and who is the lovely lassie? I have not seen this one before, but I'd wager you have already sampled her charms!" and bursting into loud laughter, had slapped Burns on the back.

He was unprepared for his friend's reaction, as he answered coldly, "I have not, then! The lass is as virtuous as she is bonnie and I'd thank you to remember that!"

Meeting the hostility is Burns face, and by the angry thrust of his chin, Hamilton realised that he had deeply offended him and was quick to make amends. He apologised handsomely, and had the good sense not to remind his friend of this oft-repeated creed, to waste no time in the pursuit of love. Burns accepted the apology and, shaking hands, made his way back to Mary.

It was a happy foursome who enjoyed their picnic, making short work of the meat pies, the bread and cheese, the honey cakes and fruit. A loud burst of hilarity from a group of young men nearby caused heads to turn and Mary blushed to see how the girls fought each other for their favours. One snatched at a lad's blue bonnet and pulled it over her head, while a rival tried to pull it off. Burns told Mary that the blue bonnets proclaimed them Weaver lads from Kilmarnock, out to enjoy a day's fun.

Mary was bewildered by all the goings-on – a woman falling off her seat, "no lass, not ill, too much drink," explained Jessie; a man raising clasped hands to heaven, begging forgiveness for his sins; everywhere a constant stumbling over feet to shouted curses and blows as men and women made their way to and from the stalls for jugs of penny-wheep and whisky-gill.

The loud ringing of a bell proclaimed the arrival of the first Minister and brought a measure of quiet to the crowded tent. Mary saw a tall, thin man with scanty white hair falling to his shoulders. This, and his white Geneva bands, was the only touch of colour in his sombre black. He mounted the steps to the dais and turned to face his audience. With both hands, he smacked the heavy Bible onto the table with a resounding thump, and when this did not bring about total silence, he motioned for the Beadle to ring his bell and at last the noise died away.

Burns whispered in Mary's ear, "It's auld Moodie. Wait you, you'll hear him howl out every sin in the Bible along with some the good Book's never listed."

John Lees leaned across Jessie. "Aye, he's well named 'Auld Nick'. Look close, lassies and you'll maybe see his horns." Jessie giggled, her face crimson from food and wine, while Mary tried to hide her shock at this miscalling of the Minister.

The Reverend Moodie began his sermon with a prayer, during which could be heard snores and drunken mutterings. The prayer ended and the real performance got under way. Suddenly, his voice rose to a shout, blaring out against all the sins of the flock, which he impressed on them by pointing to kissing couples of which there was no lack. The Reverend's passions rose to such a pitch that he stamped and leapt and howled, hurling threats of roasting pits awaiting sinners in Hell, so carried away that he did not see the sinners leaving the tent in droves.

Burns and Lees had also had enough and, gathering up their belongings, ushered Mary and Jessie outside to the fresh air.

For the rest of the day, they wandered around, listening to the wild music of the gypsy fiddlers, applauding the skill of the jugglers, laughing at the antics of the performing dogs and the dancing bears. On their way back to the cart, they stopped to look at a stall displaying china figurines, and Burns insisted on buying one for Mary, telling her, "You can't leave without a Fairing gift, not from your very first 'Holy Fair'!" Mary could not hide her pleasure as she looked at the little Shepherd boy, holding out a golden heart to his dainty Shepherdess as they sat beneath a pink-blossomed tree, a white lamb lying at their feet.

Mary lifted her eyes, to find Robert smiling down at her, and shyly, she thanked him for her Fairing, to be told that her pleasure in his gift was all that he could wish for.

When they drove away from the field, through the warm sunlight of early evening, Burns, his arm around Mary's waist, began to sing. Soon, the others joined in, and Mary, not knowing the words, hummed the tune very softly. It was a song about the Fairies and a hill of gold, with a melody pleasing to the ear, and Mary enjoyed the deep voices of the men accompanying the women's lighter tones.

When they arrived at Montgomerie, everyone was invited in to supper, and tongues wagged without pause as each one recounted what had happened at the Fair.

They were interrupted by Jean Purdie's raised voice, urging Willie to his feet. With all eyes upon him, he stood up, none too steadily, and spoke, "I . . . I have an . . . announcement to make . . . important an . . . announcement! Jean . . . Miss Purdie . . . has consented to be my wife." With a gasp of relief, he fell back onto his chair, a broad, inebriated smile on his crimson face.

After the first shock, there was an outburst of congratulations and Jean, green eyes shining at being the centre of attention for once, tossed her head and cast a look at Burns that said, "Somebody thinks me bonnie enough to marry, even if you don't."

Burns met the look and was moved to compassion. He rose to his feet and said, "I have a gift for the happy pair, and here it is." Raising his glass, he began:

> Here's to that bonnie, red-headed lass Jean,
> Nae crown does she need to make her a
>   queen:
> For Willie, sae lucky, she'll be a braw wife,
> A treasure to cherish the rest of his life.

He drained his glass to exuberant applause and John Lees was heard to remark, "It's no every lass can boast a poem from Robert Burns, Jean. Ye'll need to get him to put it in writing for ye."

Jean Purdie looked at Burns, all her animosity gone, and quietly she thanked him for his poem, knowing she would remember every word of it. Mary felt a warmth suffuse her, understanding what Robert had done, as much for her sake as his own. He had turned away Jean's spite, and made her a friend.

CHAPTER 10

Dear Friend
of my Heart

Two weeks after the Holy Fair saw the return from Edinburgh of Colonel and Mrs Montgomerie. It also saw the return of Miss Elizabeth Campbell. Within an hour, Mary received a summons to attend Miss Campbell in her sitting-room, a request that caused speculation in the kitchen, but brought no answers from Mary, who had no idea why she had been sent for.

When she arrived at the sitting-room door, she knocked quietly and entering, bent her knee in a graceful curtsey. She straightened up to find Miss Elizabeth regarding her with a displeased look on her narrow face.

"Well, Mary, and what have you to say for yourself?" As Mary in some bewilderment, remained silent, she snapped out, "Do not pretend you do not know what I mean, Miss! Stories have come to my ears that you are walking out with a Mr Robert Burns. Is that true or is it not? Please to answer me!"

Mary's gaze did not waver, as, in a steady voice she replied, "It is true that I know Mr Burns, but not true is it, to say we are walking out. Miss Smith is always present when we meet, we are never alone, and friends we are, nothing more. He has been helping me to understand this language of the Lowlands, for which I am grateful."

Mollified somewhat by Mary's obvious sincerity, the Housekeeper was still annoyed. "Jessie Smith had no right to allow this to happen! When she wrote to me, I understood it was one single meeting and I am not at all pleased! You are under my care, and I shall have to write to your parents and explain matters. Until I hear from your Father, you will see no more of Mr Burns. Do you understand?" Mary bowed her head, thankful that Robert was away from home, and hopeful that, when she talked with her Father, he would allow her to go on meeting him.

When she returned to the kitchen Jessie wanted to know what the Housekeeper had said, and Mary told her everything. Jessie seemed not to care that she was in Miss Campbell's 'bad book' and tossed her head at the ban placed on Mary's meetings with Burns. "Don't you worry, Mary. Your Father will see reason and it will all be sorted out. I will tell him myself that you've been better looked after than any Duchess, and that's the truth of it!"

When three weeks later they fianlly arrived, Elizabeth Campbell had given instructions for Mary's Father and brother to be shown immediately to her room. But Archie Campbell planned differently. He intended to hear Mary's side before listening to the Housekeeeper and so, instead of entering by the front door, he and Rab went round to the kitchen.

There was a flutter of excitement in the women gathered there when they saw the two men, one in his Captain's garb of navy-blue and gold, and young Rab in his best green broadcloth and silver buckled hat. Jessie rose to greet them, much impressed by their natural good manners

At that moment, Mary hurried in, having been fetched by an excited Effie, who was disappointed by the undemonstrative greetings exchanged by the three Campbells. She could not know that, being Highlanders, they considered any public show of emotion to be impolite, an embarrassment to them and to the onlookers.

Now Mary's Father turned to Jessie. "Mistress Smith, will you be permitting us to have a word with Mary in private, before you send word to Miss Campbell?"

"Most certainly, Captain Campbell. Mary will show you to her room."

A buzz of comment broke out when they left the kitchen. "My gracious, but isn't the Captain a handsome man?" – this from Jean Purdie. "And his son!" sighed Betty, as she recalled the merry glint in young Rab's eye, and his appreciative glance at her as he bowed. "Och, our Mary is the lucky one to have such kinfolk," came wistfully from Effie. Jessie impatiently shooed them back to work, and made up her mind to give Mary as much time as possible with her Father.

In Mary's room, Archie Campbell took his daughter into his arms and kissed her fondly, then held her from him to search her face. Smiling, Mary looked back at him, before asking shyly, "Well, Father, and have I changed in your eyes?"

Meeting her clear, guileless gaze, Archie Campbell drew a deep sigh of relief, thankful that he could see no change at all in his best-loved daughter. "The only change I see," he said as he smiled at her, "is that you are bonnier than I remember, and your Mother and I have sorely missed you."

Rab, always in a hurry, broke in. "Father, am I never to be allowed to greet my sister?" and so saying, enveloped Mary in a great hug, planting solid kisses on her cheeks.

Laughingly, Mary returned his greeting, telling him

breathlessly that he hadn't changed a bit. He was still the same 'Rab-the-Pirate' who had plagued her sorely in their youth.

Sitting beside his daughter, Archie Campbell took her hand in his and looked at her. "Mary, Miss Elizabeth has written to me of your friendship with a certain Robert Burns. Before we go to her, I would ask you this, "Is it friendship between you and nothing more?"

Mary answered her Father quietly, her blue eyes steady under his keen scrutiny. "It is friendship only, Father. Indeed, I have never had a better friend. He is helping me to understand the speech of the Lowlands, and no one teases me about being Highland when he is near."

Rab clenched his fists at this and growled, "Better to be Highland than a common Lowlander!"

"Quiet, Rab," his Father admonished him. "Let Mary continue." Mary rose to her feet and, opening a drawer, took out some pieces of paper which she placed in her Father's hand. "Robert thought of this way to help me with his language."

Archie Campbell looked at the drawing of a sheep, and Mary pointed to the three words written underneath. First was the Gaelic word, 'caora'. Next, the English word, 'sheep', followed by the Scottish word, 'yowe'. There were many more, flowers, animals, birds, all clearly drawn and clearly worded.

Before he could express his admiration, and before Rab had time to look properly at the first one, Jessie's knock on the door told them it was time to go. He held the drawings and said, "Mary, if you will allow me, I should like to show these to Elizabeth."

Miss Campbell greeted her relatives with due ceremony and bid them to be seated. She enquired after her cousin, Agnes and the other children and without more ado, opened the discussion. "Archie, you know the reason I wrote you was my concern for Mary's welfare. She has been seeing this farmer, Robert Burns of Mossgiel, though never unaccompanied and, I am certain, with no impropriety. However the young man has acquired a reputation as a philanderer, and it is this which greatly disturbs me."

Archie Campbell looked at his wife's cousin, recognising her very real concern for his daughter:. "You are right to tell me of this, Elizabeth, and I would wish to know all about the lad. Mary tells me he has become the provider for his family since his Father's death. Also it seems he is becoming known as a writer of poems and songs. If this is so, surely he has much to commend him?"

Elizabeth Campbell could not deny this, but was still not sure if it outweighed his faults.

Archie Campbell continued. "This Robert Burns is young, only a few years older than Mary, yet already he shows himself responsible and hard-working. More, he has been good to Mary." He held out the papers Mary had given him. "See, Elizabeth, how he has been helping her to learn the speech of the Lowlands."

Elizabeth Campbell looked at the drawings and looked at Mary. "Did Robert Burns draw these?" she demanded.

"Yes, Miss Elizabeth, he drew them all. I wrote the Gaelic words, and he copied them in the English and the Doric."

Rab stretched out his hand and received the papers from Miss Campbell. He exclaimed in delight at the little drawings and gave it as his opinion that, "If this Robert Burns is as clever with his writing as he is with his drawing, then his poems I should like to hear!"

Mary gave her brother a grateful look for his praise of Robert, while her Father and Miss Elizabeth came to their own agreement, which was to allow Mary to meet with Burns as long as the relationship remained one of mutual friendship only.

With a sigh of relief that the matter was settled, Miss Campbell rang the bell for tea to be brought in and graciously permitted Mary to stay and share it with them.

When the time came to say goodbye to her Father and brother, Mary had many fond wishes for her Mother and the young ones at home. It was with mixed emotions that she watched the two tall figures disappear down the drive. Part of her wished to run after them, to beg her Father to take her back with him to Campbeltown. But another part told her something quite different, that here she would stay, just to be near Robert Burns.

Two days after her Father's visit, John Lees came to Montgomerie House with a letter for Mary. With his usual fondness for making jokes, he didn't hand it over at once, but said with a deep sigh, "Och, Mary lass, I was given this letter by sic' a queer-looking gangrel body, face full o' red whiskers he had, and not a tooth in his gums. He begged me to take this message to the bonniest lass in the Big House . . ."

That was as far as he got, as an exasperated Jessie, threatening to box his ears if he didn't stop his nonsense, snatched the letter from his hand and gave it to Mary.

Just to see the handwriting brought a flutter to Mary's heart. She recognised it as Robert's, and she thrilled to the sight of her own name, Miss Mary Campbell, boldly written in black ink. Quickly, she slipped the letter into her apron-pocket, glad that Jessie was too busy giving John a tongue-wagging to notice her as she slipped out to the Dairy. Her hands flew to their task as she churned then patted the butter into her own special shapes, thistles, buttercups, ferns. Laying them on the cool, white marble shelves, she covered them with damp muslin. Now, her work done, she could escape to the thorn tree.

Seated under the drooping branches, Mary opened her letter. Carefully, she broke the thin black seal and unfolded the page. Reading the words was like hearing Robert's voice, warm and deep.

> Mary, my Dear lass,
>
> I have been away five days, and three more must pass before I see your bonnie face. The fleeting hours are ever the ones we would bid stay with us, and such I count the times shared with you beneath our Trysting tree.
>
> The business with Saint James' Lodge has taken longer than first thought, but soon I will be back at Mossgiel and my first journey will be to Montgomerie House, to see the lass whose image is ever in my heart. Till we meet, remember to 'say-me' in your prayers and that will be my sure anchor in the midst of Life's storms.
>
> Know me to be your own True Friend,
> Robert Burns.

Mary read her letter over and over, the first time slowly, trying to grasp the meaning behind the words, until finally, she understood. She whispered to herself, "I am glad that you say you are my true friend, and I will not forget to 'say-you' in my prayers."

Hearing voices, she looked out to see Jessie and

John Lees strolling along the path and hastily placing Robert's letter in her purse, she stood up and went to meet them. She was relieved that John made no reference to his absent friend and guessed that she had Jessie to thank for it.

As they walked back to Montgomerie House, she learned that Jean Purdie had named her Wedding month. "It is to be the end of September, a real 'Penny-Wedding' and the Master and Mistress have given permission for it to be in the big barn," said Jessie.

John Lees laughed, "Aye, Mary, and if you are wondering why it is so soon, maybe our Jean is feart to wait too long, in case Willie changes his mind or else dies on her and makes her a widow before she's a wife."

Jessie gave him a none too gentle push. "You have a wicked tongue, John Lees and a worse mind. Better that you curb them both before I forget my manners and warm your lugs!"

Puzzled, Mary asked, "What is this Penny Wedding, Jessie? Never have I heard of such a thing."

Jessie explained, "Each guest gives a penny to help provide a meal, and whatever else they can afford. Colonel and Mistress Montgomerie have promised a whole cow to be roasted, and barrels of ale and wine enough for all."

John Lees threw his cap in the air and jumped to catch it with a click of his heels. "It will be a night to remember, Mary, with Fiddlers to raise the roof for reels and jigs that will have the old ones hooching fit to burst!"

With a shake of the head at his foolishness, Jessie went on to tell Mary more about the Wedding. "Jean decided on September to give us a breathing space before Hallowe'en, and I must say it is real thoughtful of her, no matter what some folk might think!" – this with a hard look at John Lees, who merely pursed his lips in a shrill whistle and cast his eyes heavenwards.

Jessie explained that Jean would set up house in a cottage behind the stables, "near enough so that she can step through the gates right into the kitchen. Fine and handy for her work!"

Getting ready for bed that night, Betty was openly envious of Jean's coming Marriage and sighed, "Och, I just wish it could be me and Davie, but it will be years before we can wed. We'll have to wait until Davie gets a Head Coachman's job with rooms above the Stables." Her voice died away in a tired yawn and she lay back to dream of her Davie.

Now Mary brought out Robert's letter, to read again the words he had written, calling her his 'Dear Lass'. As she lingered over this, she was startled by Betty's voice, asking, "Mary, are you serious about Robert Burns?"

"Serious? What do you mean, Betty?" There was puzzlement in Mary's question.

"Well, I mean, I don't want you to get hurt when you find out things. He has lots o' lassies, and there is talk of one at Mossgiel . . ."

Here she was stopped by Mary, saying in a voice she had never before used, so cold and distant was it. "I am not wishing to hear you Betty. Robert Burns is my friend, and those who speak against him speak with ill tongues. I will bid you goodnight."

Betty, who had spoken only for Mary's good, was so crushed she could find nothing to say.

Mary's rare anger vanished as she said her prayers and, ashamed of speaking so to Betty, she asked forgiveness before she too slept.

CHAPTER 11
Beneath the Hawthorn Tree

When John Lees next brought news from Robert Burns, it was by word-of-mouth, asking Mary to wait for him beneath the Hawthorn tree on the next Sunday evening.

Before giving Mary the message, John asked for a word with the Cook, and his serious demeanour so alarmed Jessie that she instantly took him into the pantry and closed the door. "Well," she demanded, "out with it, man. Something's wrong, and if it concerns Mary and Robert Burns, you had better tell me what he's been up to!"

Glancing at Jessie's scarlet cheeks and hard-closed mouth, Lees told her nervously, "Och, Jessie, it is maybe nothing at all. You know Robert was friendly with Lizzie Paton before he met with Mary?" And at Jessie's explosive outburst he hurried on "well, see you, he has been out with her a few times, hardly surprising and her servant to his Mother at Mossgiel, but I'm thinking maybe it's gone a wee bittie further than might be thought wise."

Jessie, breathing heavily, strong white teeth biting her lower lip, for a moment could find no words.

Looking at her sideways, with some apprehension, he asked, "Think you to have a word in Mary's ear? Or, maybe better to let sleeping dogs lie?" Jessie considered this, remembering Betty's account of Mary's cold displeasure at her own attempt to warn her of Burns' many affairs.

"No," she decided. "Mary and Robert are only friends, as she has told her Father and she will hear no ill of him. And when all is said and done, better to seek his pleasures with servant lassies at Mossgiel than to try such tricks here."

John Lees, much relieved at Jessie's decision, gave Mary the message from Burns, and set aside his doubts. He told himself that Robert could put forward his own case, with his ever-eloquent tongue as persuasive as the poems and songs which flowed from him so effortlessly.

When Jessie and Mary reached the thorn tree that Sunday evening, it was to find Burns and Lees rounding the path from the Faile. On catching sight of them Robert and John swept off their hats to flourish them exuberantly in the air, at the same time quickening their steps almost to a run, with Robert's longer legs putting him in the lead. Mary and Jessie could not refrain from laughing as they waited for the young men to reach them. Robert sketched a deep bow, giving himself time to get his breath back and, straightening up, had the presence of mind to greet Jessie first before his eager gaze fastened on Mary's smiling face.

Turning to Jessie and John, his look asked them to leave him alone with Mary. John Lees opened his mouth to utter a remark about all sitting down together, but a warning glance from Robert stopped him. He knew better that to take liberties when Burns was in this mood, and smoothly, he changed his words to say, "Well, Mary, if you will excuse us, we'll just take a dander as far as the bridge." And taking Jessie's arm, he walked with her down the path.

The Love of Highland Mary

When Mary seated herself beneath the tree, Burns stood for a moment looking down at her. He gazed at her face as if he could never have his fill of it, seeing the dimple in her cheek, the red lips curving in a smile, the clear eyes, so deeply blue, looking at him without guile. Impulsively he spoke.

"Mary, I have missed you! When noisy clacking tongues wearied me, the thought of you was like a cup of cold water in a desert place."

Throwing himself down at her side, he reached out for her hand, spreading the slender fingers apart to press against his own square palm and, as like draws to like, they meshed together in a silent bonding. Drawing a deep breath, Burns said, "Mary, John tells me that you have had a visit from your Father. Does he know about me?"

Quietly Mary answered, "Yes, Robert, he knows."

Urgently now, Burns wanted to know, "And does he approve?" Mary leaned back against the tree and smiled reassuringly, "Robert, I am here with you, and that must tell you I have my Father's approval. And my brother's!" Mary spoke the last words with held-in merriment and in his relief, Burns laughed aloud.

"Rab-the-Pirate! I am glad he is not against me, but what weighed with him in my favour?"

Smiling, Mary told him, "he liked your way of teaching me your language and said if your poems match your pictures, then it is a genius you are."

"And your Father, what conditions did he set out for our meetings?"

"Just that there should always be others present, and that we remain friends and nothing more."

A shadow darkened Burns's face at this. "Ah, then perhaps he has heard rumours about me? Rumours which name me as a womaniser, a hell-raiser?"

Mary raised her head to say proudly, "my Father would pay no head to rumours! No more do I. Friendship that is true means trusting and accepting the whole being of your friend, asking no questions of his life apart."

Burns regarded Mary, a strange mixture of emotions flitting over his face, the main one being wonder. For the first time in his life, he was with a young woman who asked of him no more than friendship whilst giving him her complete trust in return. Quietly, sincerely, he said now, "Mary, I am truly honoured by your words, and your Father will never have cause to rue his trust in me, nor will you."

Taking both her hands in his, he held them tight as he looked deep into her eyes. "As you are my true friend, so I am yours, and our friendship is a thing most precious to me, my own dear lass."

For a few moments they sat quietly together, happy in each other's company, needing no words to express their feelings. Jessie's voice and John's laughter brought them out of their dreams, telling them it was time to return to Montgomerie.

Walking together, for the first time Mary, of her own accord, took Robert's arm and felt him press it close to his side as be bent his head to smile down at her blushing face, but said no word to embarrass her.

The following Sunday was a disappointing one for both Mary and Jessie, as neither Robert Burns nor John Lees was in Church. In the afternoon, seeing that Mary was restless and unsettled, Jessie suddenly said, "Go and put your bonnet on, Mary! We're going for a walk."

Mary's face brightened and she hurried to do as she was told. The day was cool, with a fresh wind blowing, and Jessie took Mary's arm with one hand while holding onto her bonnet with the other, gasping out, "Mercy on us, it would need more than ribbons to hold our hats on in this wind!"

But Mary lifted her face to its keen buffeting and felt her spirits rise as the autumn leaves danced widdershins around her. When they reached the bridge, the wind was at their back, forcing them to run so that their feet hardly touched the wooden planks. They were on the far bank before Jessie got her breath back. She straightened her bonnet, tucking in strands of hair which had fallen over her eyes, urging Mary to do likewise and appear 'decent-like' on the Lord's day, and not like a 'pair of tinks'.

As they came to a fork in the road, Jessie was thankful they had tidied themselves, for approaching them were two young men, each leading a prancing horse.

The girls immediately recognised Robert Burns and John Lees and Jessie called out, "Well, well! If it isn't our absent friends!"

When he heard this, Burns turned to look, and on seeing Mary, his face lit up in a delighted smile as he said, "Mary Lass! And Jessie. I had not hoped to see you this day. John here is helping me get this pair back to Mossgiel, as I am on my own. My family are all in Ayr visiting relations, which is the reason I was not at the Kirk." Lees had no chance to say anything as he tried to hold onto the reins while his horse danced sideways and tossed it's head, heeding not John's shouted commands to "steady on!" and "stand still, ye daft beast!"

The onlookers could not keep from laughing, and Burns said, "After all John's hard work, he is in sore need of refreshment!" And turning to Mary, he proferred an invitation "Would you and Jessie come and take tea with us? Then I could show you around the farm?"

Mary bit her lip uncertainly and looked to Jessie for

guidance and the Cook's natural curiosity to see Mossgiel farm brought her answer. "We'd be delighted, Robert, I'm sure."

With reins in one hand, and Mary's arm in the other, Burns led the way, John following with Jessie. When they walked up the incline, past fields of new-cut oats, a trim, white-washed farm house came into view, with large barn, stables and byres.

Mary exclaimed in approval, "Why, Robert, it is a fine place you have here, everything so well-kept that it is much to your credit."

Opening the door of his house, Robert stepped aside for them to enter. They saw a large, black-raftered room, lit by a burning, red-flamed fire in a shining black-leaded range.

Jessie and Mary noted the scarlet geraniums on the window-sill, the handsomely carved chairs and long settle, the tea-things laid out on the refectory table where a vase of crimson rosehip berries cast their reflection on the mirrored surface.

Leaving John to entertain Mary and Jessie, Burns made the tea, set out a tray of scones and handed them round, as Jessie told him, "as well as I could have done myself."

When they had finished their tea, Burns showed them over the farm, ending up at a field bordering the road to Montgomerie. Smiling at Mary, he led her a little way off from the others, speaking softly so that only she could hear. "Look closely, Mary at this very special place. It was here that John brought me the news I most wanted to hear."

Mary looked at him, wondering what he meant, and he went on. "He told me that a certain lovely lass at Montgomerie House went by the name of Mary

Campbell, that she was not walking-out with any lad, and that I was soon to meet her.

At this Mary's soft laughter dimpled her cheeks and she said, "Why, Robert, that is not so very long ago, and yet, it seems to me that always I have known you."

Burns would have said more, but had no time as Jessie and Lees moved over to join them. Jessie asked about his harvest and he shook his head. "Not good, Mossgiel is too high up, with soil too thin and stony, so that it yields but poor crops." Then he apologised, saying, "But forgive my bad manners, inflicting on you such talk. I will not be a farmer forever, and one day, instead of the plough, I will earn my livelihood with my pen."

Mary looked at him questioningly, and he explained, "My friend Gavin Hamilton, the man you saw at the Fair, has asked me to compile a book of poems and songs, and when it is published, I will turn over my share of Mossgiel to my brother Gilbert."

His three companions looked at him with mixed feelings, Lees with unstinted admiration and conviction of his success, Jessie with a deal of scepticism that he might be too optimistic, Mary with sudden insight, which told her it would be as he said, that fame and fortune would come to him through his poems and songs.

Soon after this, Jessie reluctantly decided they would have to start back to Montgomerie, and Burns and Lees proposed to escort them as far as the bridge. Strolling along, arm-in-arm with Mary, he told her he had heard of Jean Purdie's coming Wedding, and asked, "Will you be my partner, lass? At the Wedding and at the dancing."

Mary looked up at him, hesitating as to how she should answer and he, hurt, wanted to know her reason. "Do you not want to partner me, Mary? Or is it you have someone else in mind?"

At the note of chagrin in his voice, Mary hastened to reassure him. "No, no, Robert, that is not so. It is only that I do not know how to dance and fear to disappoint you in front of all your friends."

In his relief, Burns laughed aloud before saying tenderly, "Is that all you fear, my bonnie lass? You will never disappoint me over so light a cause. We will dance or not dance. It shall be just as you wish." They said their goodbyes at the bridge, with Burns and Lees promising to attend the Penny Wedding the following week, John making jokes about having to borrow a penny from Jessie, who tossed her head and disdained to reply to his nonsense.

That night, Mary dreamed of dancing with Robert to the lively music of the Fiddles, his strong arm guiding her surely in all the steps. So happy was she in her dreaming that, when she woke up, she kept the happiness with her and longed for the coming Wedding.

CHAPTER 12

The Penny Wedding

The day before the Wedding, Mary put the finishing touches to her gift for the bride. It was a creamy lace fichu, fine as a cobweb, to cover the shoulders before falling into three delicate frills. Carefully, she carried it down to the kitchen, where Jean and Jessie were busy sorting out dishes of cakes, sweetmeats, scones and little baskets of raisins.

Effie, thinking herself unseen, took advantage of Mary's entrance to stuff a sweetmeat into her mouth and promptly received a box on the ears, with a warning that she'd be locked in her room all the next day with no chance to enjoy the festivities. Knowing Jessie would be as good as her word, Effie broke into noisy howls, which only stopped when she saw Mary's gift. At sight of which Jean and Jessie exclaimed with pleasure.

Jean wiped her hands carefully on a clean white cloth before taking the fichu from Mary, and looking at it, she said, "It is the bonniest thing I've ever seen, Mary. I . . . I do not know how to thank you."

Jessie tore her gaze away from the filmy lace to join her praises. "Jean has the right of it, lass! Words fail me, that they do."

Blushing to hear them, Mary gently arranged the collar over Jean's shoulders, saying, "If I see it on you now, I can better tell how it will look tomorrow."

Effie, eyes big as saucers, could not keep quiet. "Och, Jean, it makes your face awful bonnie, just like a real bride. See!" She darted to the mantelpiece, snatched down a thick square of mirrored glass, and held it up to Jean.

Looking into the mirror, Jean Purdie saw herself transformed. The cream of the lace gave her sallow skin the shine of buttermilk, deepened the green of her eyes to emerald and changed her red hair to sunset gold.

Jessie, head to one side, scrutinised her thoughtfully as Mary's skilful fingers arranged the frills in symmetrical order. Suddenly, she made up her mind. "I think I know just what's needed to set it off! I noticed some tea-roses blooming in the garden, with plenty of buds still on them." She turned to Effie. "Your job will be to bring in half-a-dozen of the best buds with enough stems to pin them over the frills. Do you think you could manage that, lass?"

Effie's thin little face lit up and she clasped her hands in delight at being made a part of the Wedding. "Och aye, Cook! I'll go out and cut them while they're fresh, and . . . and I'll shake off the dewdrops so as not to mark the bonnie lace."

Mary smiled approval at Jessie's kind act, and Jessie, to cover up her feelings, produced a box which she handed to Jean. "Here's my gift, Jean. You can use it to fasten the roses to your dress."

Jean opened the box and drew out a round, gilt brooch, set with a pale, yellow topaz. Silently, she held the dainty trinket in her hand, and when she looked at Jessie, there were tears in her eyes. "It's far too good for me, Jessie, but I thank you and I will be proud to wear it. See how braw it looks on Mary's kerchief." And she held it so that the topaz shone gold against the creamy lace.

The Love of Highland Mary

Effie broke the tension by jumping up and down, clapping her hands and crying out, "Och, Jean, I wish I was a bride wi' such finery to wear to my Wedding!"

Looking at the skinny figure, all eyes in a pointed face, the idea of her as a bride made them break into laughter, which did not daunt Effie one whit as she laughed with them.

No one expected to sleep that night, but worn out with all the preparations, they, and the house, settled into the hush of exhaustion. At cock-crow, Mary and Betty awoke. It was their task to help the bride get ready, while Jessie prepared the meal for everyone before they set out for the Church.

As they dressed, Effie came in with a cluster of deep cream rosebuds and Mary gave her some yellow ribbons, showing her how to wrap them around the stems.

They had no need to wake Jean. She was up before them, brushing out her red hair and pinning it in coils over each ear.

When Betty helped fasten her green, woollen dress, Mary was ready with the collar. She placed it so that the points ended in the jabot of frills and spoke over her shoulder to Effie, saying, "Come now, Effie, and bring to me the roses." She centred the cluster, and pinned it carefully with the topaz brooch. Stepping back to look, she nodded her approval, "Lovely you are, Jean, a lovely bride for your bride-groom." As they went down to breakfast, Jean was anxious to know if there would be enough food and drink for the celebrations, saying anxiously, "For it is black affrontit I will be if it runs out."

Mary reassured her. "So much food I have never in my life seen. The tables in the barn are all covered with meats, cakes and I know not what all is there. Is that not so, Betty?"

"Aye, it is so! And drink? Barrels and barrels of drink, enough to drown an army!"

Effie wanted to know, "But can a penny a head pay for all that?"

"No, it cannot!" she was told by Betty. "The Elders say that a penny is enough for a Wedding feast, but those that can afford it pay a lot more, and of course the Colonel and the Mistress are supplying the roast meats and the ale and wine."

Breakfast over, the women went off to finish their dressing, tidying hair, fixing bonnets, gathering up purses and posies. That done, they gathered outside in the garden to wait for the men.

Mary was glad that the day was fair, with no cloud to mar the pale blue sky and only the lightest breeze to rustle the branches. Betty nudged her arm and pointed to the men making their way towards them. Foremost among them was one they hardly recognised, so fine was he in his maroon-caped coat, tall black hat with silver buckle, and highly polished black leather topboots.

Effie, in new pink dress and straw bonnet, gave a startled shriek, "It's Willie! Oh, isn't he the braw bridegroom!"

Jean evidently thought so, and proudly took his arm to lead the procession to the Kirk. Dancing in front went the youngest lads and lasses, holding long ropes of ribbons and flowers, and passing comments that would have brought them swift punishment had their elders been closer at hand.

As Mary, Jessie and Betty walked together, Jessie remarked, "I hope Willie and Jean know their Ten Commandments, because if they don't, old Daddy Auld is like to stop the Wedding and tell them to come back better prepared."

Betty giggled. "I'd like to see him try that on Jean! She'd not hesitate to fleg him! Besides, the Colonel and the Mistress will be there, with a fat purse for him and a feast to follow."

As they entered the Church, Mary's eye was caught by a tall figure in dark blue coat and white breeches. She heard Jessie exclaim, "It's Robert Burns, and there's John Lees! He told me they were only coming to the Dancing!"

A pink blush coloured Mary's cheeks as she met Robert's smiling gaze, and she was unable to hide her delight as he and John came over to claim their seats beside them.

Throughout the ceremony, Mary heard only snatches, " . . . gathered together in the sight of God to join this man and this woman in Holy Matrimony," and " . . . Marriage is a Sacrament," . . . "and no man shall sever God's union."

With the warmth of Robert's arm against her own, Mary was unaware of the long drawn-out sermon, and was startled by the noisy closing of the heavy, brass-bound Bible as the service was brought to an end. So great was the crowd thronging the road that Burns was able to hold Mary's hand in his without attracting attention.

He looked down at her and said, "Well, Mary lass, I wonder what you will think of Jean's Penny Wedding? When we dance to the Fiddles, you will dance only with me! John Lees has been saying he would like to take you up in a Reel, but he had better not try it!"

Mary, still unsure of her ability to pick up the proper steps, was glad that Robert would be there to help her, and had no wish to partner anyone else.

When they entered the big, spacious barn, they saw the long tables sagging under the weight of all the food, with barrels against the wall, filled with beer, ale and wine. Colonel Montgomerie, moustache bristling, wished Willie and Jean happiness in their wedded life, as did Mrs Montgomerie.

Everyone raised their glasses to toast the Bride and Groom, after which the Colonel and his Lady took their leave. This was the signal for the real festivities to begin and the drink to flow, while the musicians tuned up their fiddles.

Willie and Jean led off the dancing, squaring up to each other in a lively Jig, fingers snapping, as they linked arms in a fast-moving pattern, interspersed with loud 'hoochs'.

Soon, others joined in, and wilder grew the leaps and jumps, and louder rose the cries of the dancers.

Mary and Robert watched and laughed at the antics, while Robert's fingers and feet beat time to the music. Suddenly he rose, drawing Mary to her feet, saying, "Come, Lass, it is time for your first lesson."

With no time to be alarmed, Mary found herself on the floor where, guided expertly by Robert, she was soon following his steps in the dance. A couple whirled by, and they saw it was Effie and Jimmie, the latter somewhat the worse for an over-supply of drink. Burns called out, "Careful, Effie lass, else you'll have Jimmie tapsalteerie!" When they resumed their seats, Mary was glad of the chance to get her breath back and to quench her thirst with a glass of cold buttermilk.

A sudden commotion at the entrance to the barn caused heads to turn as two young women thrust themselves noisily into the midst of the dancers.

Jessie, partnering John Lees, had her back to them, and she heard his exclamation as he stared over her shoulder, "Dod Almighty, it's Lizzie Paton!"

When she heard this, Jessie whirled round as though stung by a wasp. She saw the woman, evidently the worse for drink, hair hanging in wisps over her scarlet face, her open bodice revealing over-much flesh, eyes searching the tables and fixing on the one where Burns sat with Mary.

Prevented by the crush of people on the floor from reaching them, she struck out wildly, yelling, "There ye are, Master Burns, an' is this the Hieland stoat that's been keepin' ye oot o' ma bed at nicht?"

Her companion tried to hush her up, pawing her arm and crying, "Haud yer tongue, Lizzie, and come awa' oot o' this. It's no richt tae cause sic a stushie at a weddin'."

Robert Burns, thankful that most of the folk were too drunk to bother with Lizzie, rose to his feet and pushed his way through the revellers till he reached her. He spoke no word, but the look on his face was enough to silence the rest of Lizzie's furious words. Taking her by the arm, he led her outside, followed by the unsteady Beenie who, eager to escape Burns's anger, was gabbling to him, "Ach, Rob, she's awfu' drunk, dinnae be too sair on her." Burns paid her no heed, concentrating his mind on the now wordless Lizzie, as he wondered what to do with her. Seen in the clear light, she was a sorry-looking creature. One glance she darted at Burns before lowering her head to stare at the ground.

She heard him ask quietly, "What made you do it, lassie? It's not like you to carry-on like a tinker."

The concern in his voice and her shame at what she had done brought moisture to Lizzie's eyes and a lump to her throat. Dumbly, she shook her head from side-to-side, then the dam broke and she sobbed loudly as the tears poured down her cheeks. "Be . . . because you've

stopped comin' to me at nicht and I cannae bear it! Ah
wid raither dee!"

The real agony in her voice moved Burns to deep
pity, and he felt a sick disgust at himself for being the
cause of it. Wanting to spare her from the eyes and ears
of onlookers, he led her away from the barn to the shelter
of some nearby trees. Taking out his handkerchief, he
dried her face and smoothed her hair into a semblance of
neatness.

Under his ministrations, Lizzie's sobs died away,
and with a final gasping little hiccough, she pressed his
hand to her lips and whispered, "Och, Robbie, it's sorry
I am to have shamed you in front o' your fine friends,
but . . . but it's because I'm feart, feart oot o' ma wits!"

At her words, Burns felt a cold prickle at the back
of his neck and, carefully, he put the question to her.
"Frightened, lass? Of what?"

Head drooping, Lizzie blurted out the words he did
not want to hear. "Ah'm goin' to have a bairn, your bairn,
Robbie, and ah'm feart ye'll turn me oot o' Mossgiel."

When his first shock subsided, he experienced a
totally unexpected emotion at the thought of the coming
child, his child! and he wanted it. This was the thing that
surprised him.

Lizzie, afraid of his silence, stammered, "Ah . . . ah
could go tae auld Jinty, but ah dinnae hae the sillar."

Burns gripped her arms and said sternly, "You are
not to go near that woman. She is not to be trusted. Now
pay heed, you will not be put out of Mossgiel, but will be
looked after until your time comes. My Mother will look
after the bairn, and you will get a dowry to set you up
with a likely lad."

Calling to Beenie, Burns saw them on their way,
and knew that his decision to look after Lizzie and his

unborn child was the right one. As he made his way back to the barn, his mind was preoccupied by what he would say to Mary, and how she would react. To keep her friendship was uppermost in his thoughts, and he knew he could not bear it if she turned away from him.

Seeing the grim set to his mouth, John Lees passed him a brimming tankard of ale, his hand unsteady from his own copious drinking, while Jessie's crimson cheeks told of the many glasses of wine she had imbibed.

Mary's eyes met his, their steady gaze reassuring, and Burns felt an upsurge of relief to find no condemnation. When he started to explain, Mary gently shook her head, saying, "It is all right Robert. John has told me about the young woman. I hope you saw to her safe journey home."

Burns leaned over to take her hand, and said, "Yes, lass, that I did, and one thing more I must say. My association with her was brief and of little account, and ended before I ever met you, but the result of it will be mine to bear, and I will take care of it. Do you understand?"

Steadfastly, Mary returned his look and steadfastly she answered his question. "I understand, Robert, and respect you for it." That was all she said, and Burns knew he need explain no further.

As the dancers gyrated madly to the wild screeching of the fiddles, Burns shepherded Mary out of the barn, closely followed by the stumbling John and Jessie.

When they reached Montgomerie House, the first pale stars were shining in the twilight sky. A cool breeze made Mary shiver, and seeing this, Robert took John by the arm and bid her and Jessie goodnight. For once it was Mary who had to take charge of the Cook, who was still unsteady on her feet. Seating her at the table, Mary brewed the tea and put a steaming, sweetened cup in her hand, urging her to drink it while it was still hot. When she had done so, she staggered to her room, with Mary to help her undress, and was fast asleep the moment her head touched the pillow.

Mary was awakened by the noisy return of the revellers, hearing Effie's voice shrilling above the rest, "Och, whit a great weddin' it's been, but dae ye ken, the best thing ah like is Hallowe'en an' that's still to come!"

Turning over on her side, Mary smiled, remembering that Robert had promised to make her a turnip lantern to "frighten away the bogles." Her last conscious thought, before sleep overcame her, was of Robert, as he would be her first thought when she awoke.

CHAPTER 13

Hallowe'en

After a long spell of mist and rain, the end of October turned fine and sunny, to the relief of everyone at Montgomerie House.

To Mary, it meant that she could look forward once again to meeting Robert under the thorn tree, now that the Faile was no longer in spate and the roads no longer knee deep in mud.

Setting out with Jessie that Sabbath afternoon, Mary breathed in the scent of brambles and moist earth, so warmed by the sun that steam rose up in a pungent cloud.

Both Jessie and Mary wore heavy woollen cloaks which, before they had travelled any distance, became too hot for comfort. With one accord, they stopped to take them off, and Jessie exclaimed, "Who would have thought the weather could have changed so quickly! Weeks of wind and gales and worse, mists that hid everything from sight."

Mary, draping her blue cloak over her arm, said, "It is the first time my cloak has been truly dry and 'tis myself thinks my bones are drying also. Like an old woman I have been feeling."

Jessie, red cheeks aglow, studied Mary as they walked on, admiring the tall, slender figure, the golden hair curling under the blue bonnet, the pink cheeks and deep-blue eyes shining as she lifted her face to the sun.

"Is that so, Mary? Well, I can tell you that is not

how you look. I did take heed that you've maybe seemed a wee bit droopy, but have no doubt it was the lack o' seein' Robert that ailed you." Mary's cheeks flushed from pink to rose, and to hide her blushes she turned aside to pick a cluster of crimson berries from the hedge. Laughing, Jessie took her by the arm and led her along the path, saying, "You'll need to peek into the looking-glass on Hallowe'en night, Mary, if you want to see the face of the man you will wed."

"What is this you are saying, Jessie? That I can see such a thing just by looking into a glass?"

Hurriedly Jessie told her, "No, no, not at all. It is a thing of magic, but here are the lads and whatever you do, don't say a word to Robert. It is a thing for the lassies only. But I will tell you more later."

In her happiness at seeing Robert, Mary forgot all about the looking-glass, and when they were seated beneath the tree, they were content to look into each others eyes with no need for words.

At last, Robert reached out to place a gentle finger on Mary's cheek, sighing, "Now I know you are real, and I am not dreaming! Tell me you have missed me, Mary, for I have sorely felt the want of you."

With no coyness, in all sincerity, Mary told him what he wanted to hear, adding, "I feared the rain would never stop and oh, the days and nights were long and wearisome, waiting on word from you."

"Ye cannot know how I have longed to be with you, my dear lass, for true it is that when I am with you, my common self disappears and I am a different man – a better man!"

There was no mistaking the ring of truth in his voice, nor the sincerity in his eye as they gazed earnestly into hers, and Mary felt happy to know that she had too much influence over his volatile, passionate nature. She quivered at the touch of his warm lips as he pressed a kiss into the palm of her hand, and he, aware of this, instantly released her and began to speak of the coming festivities.

"My Mother's old servant used to have us scared to death with her stories of witches and warlocks, and black cats as big as panthers with blazing eyes, and wailing ghosts rising out of graves and floating down the streets! But don't you have the same customs in the Highlands?"

Mary shook her head, "No, we do not, though, to be sure, we have fierce creatures like the Water Kelpies. They are horses, sometimes black, sometimes white, who appear in rich saddles and bridles, to lure wealthy travellers to their death."

Burns, his interest aroused, wanted to know all about the Kelpies, and Mary began the story of a man whose horse had bolted, meeting up with a truly magnificent black stallion, decked out in scarlet and gold harness, with silver rings that made fine music. Grazing quietly on the grass, the animal moved closer and closer, until it was at his side. Hardly able to believe his luck, the man mounted and took up the reins to a jingling of bells. At once the Kelpie flew away like the wind, neighing horribly and almost riding in the air.

The unlucky traveller, clinging desperately to its flowing mane, could be heard crying and pleading for help. Only one man of the village, brave enough to risk peering through a crack in his shuttered window, saw the flaring scarlet nostrils, the huge white teeth, the blazing eyes, and witnessed the Demon Kelpie plunge into the black loch and sink out of sight, with the terrified man's cries still rending the air. The hapless traveller was never seen again.

Burns, spellbound by the savage drama of the tale, declared, "Mary, your Water Kelpie is far more terrifying a creature than all our ghosts and witches!"

But Mary shivered and told him, "All unnatural things are to be feared, Robert, and I like them not."

"But see you, Mary lass, Hallowe'en is a night for fun, and while the lassies squeal and pretend to be scared, it is so that the lads will act as their protectors. Now, give me a smile, my bonnie dear, and let me see the roses bloom on your cheeks, else I'll be getting the sharp edge of Jessie's tongue, for here she comes at a fine canter!" Mary laughed and sighed in the one breath, thinking, regretfully, how swiftly the time had gone.

The last day of October fell that year on a Friday, which everyone agreed was great good luck. Seeing Mary's puzzlement, Betty explained, "If it had been a Saturday, we'd not have been able to celebrate properly, because midnight would have been the Sabbath."

On the Friday afternoon. preparations were under way for the Hallowe'en party and Effie was so excited she could hardly keep still. Running to empty her apronful of red apples into a basket, she spilled them instead onto the floor, where they rolled and bumped all over the stone flags. Her shrill squeals of dismay brought Jessie to the scene and her brawny arm shot out and missed as Effie stooped to scuttle after the fallen fruit.

Helpless with laughter, Betty and Mary joined in Effie's chase after the apples, while a fuming Jessie ordered them to let the hapless limmer set her own carelessness to rights.

Mary brought in baskets of glossy brown hazelnuts and was told to place them by the fire, but not so close that they started jumping too soon. Effie told Mary, "We're to have sowen's for supper, and seein' it is

Hallowe'en, we'll sup them wi' butter, and no wi' milk." She explained that sowens was meal cooked and mixed with honey into a porridge-like gruel and smacked her lips at the thought of the treat to come.

Next, Mary went to help Jessie stack candles on a table outside the larder door, one candle to each lass, as they sought to see into their future. Inside there was no window and no light, save the glimmer from a slab of mirrored glass set on a shelf. Jessie's words had made Mary shiver, and silently resolve to have no part in it.

"You come in here, alone, with a lighted candle in one hand and an apple in the other, and say, as you look into the mirror, 'show me the face of the one I will wed, as he looks o'er my shoulder, 'tis he I will bed'. And you must take a bite from your apple between each word."

When Mary asked what would happen if no image appeared in the glass, she was told that meant the lass would never find a husband. As they set out the last of the candles, Effie crept at their heels, whispering fearfully, "I mind the story o' Mysie Grant. 'Twas said when she looked in the mirror, she saw Auld Nick! She came runnin' oot, crazed oot o' her wits, screamin' aboot the black face wi' horns and fire spewin' frae its mooth!"

Mary shivered, feeling the goose-bumps rise on her arms, but Jessie exclaimed robustly, "Havers, Effie! Just pure havers! Some o' the lads must have played a trick on her and she was too feeble minded to know it."

Effie was not convinced, saying doubtfully, "Well ah dinnae ken, Ah'd like to see the lad ah'm tae marry, but ah'd be feart to go in by masel'."

Jessie declared she had heard enough of such nonsense and threatened dire consequences if she didn't hold her tongue.

By seven o'clock, everything was ready. Jessie's high

wooden chair, padded with soft cushions, was set beside the glowing fire, not for Jessie, but for old Grannie Urquhart. Hallowe'en was to be her night, when she would order the ceremonies, interpret the signs and portents, read palms and tell the future.

At half-past seven, Mary looked through the window to see if anyone was coming, and drew in a breath of delight at the scene which met her eyes. Shining along the roadway was a long line of bobbing golden lights, and as they came closer, she saw that they were lanterns, carved from turnips into faces with round eyes and grinning mouths through which shone the yellow lights of candles.

Striding in front was a tall, wide-shouldered man, leading a sturdy pony on which was perched a very small figure. Mary blinked her eyes and called Jessie to come and look, exclaiming, "Surely he cannot be bringing such a young child so late at night! It is not seemly!"

Jessie stared, and then broke into a loud laugh. "'Tis no child, Mary, 'tis Granny Urquhart and her son Big John. Come quick, we must be at the door to bid them welcome."

Jessie, Mary and all the men and women of the House, gathered in a group to do honour to the 'Queen' of Hallowe'en.

John Urquhart reached out to lift his Mother into his arms and, in a circle of lanterns, he carried her to the door. Jessie curtsied low, then stepped aside, saying, "Mistress Urquhart, we bid you welcome to Montgomerie House. Please to enter in."

So fascinated was Mary at the sight of the little, muffled figure, that she failed to see Robert in the forefront of the watchers. True to his promise, he had brought her a lantern cut from the biggest, roundest turnip he could find. Now he followed close behind as Grannie Urquhart was divested of her shawls and settled amongst the cushions in front of the glowing range.

Mary saw a tiny, old woman in a frilled, white mutch tied with ribbons beneath the chin. The face that peered forth was as brown and wrinkled as a walnut, with a toothless mouth and eyes as bright and sharp as a squirrels. In a surprisingly strong voice, she demanded that her son fetch a stool for her dangling feet that reached only half-way to the floor. Jessie brought her a tankard of hot wine, honey and whisky, and the old woman supped it with noisy appreciation.

Taking advantage of the moment, Robert covered Mary's eyes and whispered in her ear, "Name the lad behind you, and be sure you name him right."

Mary put her hands over his, and said in the Gaelic, "Raibeart".

Laughing, he turned her to face him, saying in a mock-ferocious growl, "Had you named another, it would have been a duel at dawn!" Then holding her fast at his side, he said, "Look closely, Mary, and tell me what you see."

Mary gazed around her, at the giggling lassies in their ribbons and fal-de-rals, the lads in their finest coats and breeches, at the red and yellow flames of the fire, at Old Grannie Urquhart, and looked again to exclaim in surprise. "Why, Robert, she is smoking a pipe!"

Burns laughter rang out. "Aye, she is indeed. See how lustily she sucks the smoke up the stem, then blows it out into a cloud that hides her face!"

A sudden noise pulled them about, and they looked to see Grannie rapping her mug on the arm of her chair. She gestured to everyone to draw near, and like flies to honey they gathered round her. Twosomes, like Mary and Robert, stood close together; others, like Effie, sat on the floor as near to Grannie's chair as they could get.

The little, wrinkled face turned this way and that, as the bright eyes observed the expressions of wonderment, excitement, timidity, boldness and shrinking fearfulness. She held up a finger and said, "It's time to begin, if ye'd be home before midnight, for that's the time when the graves open and the dead rise up, and terrible will be the deeds they perform in the Kirkyard. Auld Nick will be there, black as soot, playing his fiery bagpipes for the unholy ones, and they screechin' and skirlin', jumpin' and lowpin' with their grave-clothes flyin' like gypsies tatters. Ye must never gang near, else ye'll be dragget doon to the deepest grave without even a coffin about ye."

Grannie, a born storyteller, delivered this warning in a quavery, whispery voice that raised goose-bumps on arms and necks and brought from the crouching Effie a stifled shriek of pure terror. Ignoring her, the old woman went on, "The first thing to be done is the pulling of the kail-stocks. Ye must go out in two's, holding hands and with your eyes shut, and each pull up a stock. Bring them here to me and I'll tell your fortune. Away ye go now, the lot of ye, and mind, nae keeking!"

Robert and Mary led the way to the kailyard where, by torch, they felt for the stocks and pulled them from the damp earth. In the darkness around them, other couples stumbled, giggling, as they too gathered their stocks and fell in behind Robert and Mary.

Holding fast to Robert's hand as to an anchor, Mary felt her heart beating madly. She sensed that Grannie Urquhart's powers went beyond simple fortune-telling, and suddenly she knew that she did not want to see into the future. Surreptitiously, she let the kail-stock drop from her hand onto the path, where it was trampled into the ground and lost.

They stood in front of the old woman, who looked at Mary's empty hands and nodded her head till the frills on her mutch danced round her face. She said, slowly, "Aye, lassie, ye have brought no fortune to be read, but mayhaps 'tis for a reason." Swift and keen, her eyes lifted to Mary's before she turned to Burns. Taking the kail-stock from him, she examined the earth that clung to its roots. "There is siller here, and here, see you, but at the end it is bare, no more gold."

She looked into the fire, lost in thought, until suddenly her head lifted and her eyes rested full on Burns, "There's love to come, and love to go, and beyond love is a shining and a darkness." She snatched up his right hand and peered at it, then did the same to Mary, before placing them palm-to-palm within her own. She held them enclosed for a brief moment, then freed them and said no more as she turned away.

Somehow, Grannie's separating of their hands held a significance for Mary that troubled her, though she could neither understand nor explain it. She heard Robert say, "That was a queer-like fortune auld Grannie gave me, not easy to make out, so better forgotten!" Then he asked, "Mary, why did you not tell me you had dropped your kail-stock? We could have gone back for another." Now Mary was able to smile at him as she confessed she had lost it on purpose.

Burns was surprised to hear her say so, asking her, "Don't you want to know your fortune? If that is true, you must be the only lass here who doesn't." Then, teasingly, he whispered in her ear, "Or is it that you are waiting to look in the mirror for a glimpse of your sweetheart? I tell you this, lass, if you see any other face but mine, that lying mirror will not last an instant!"

Truthfully, Mary told him that she would see no one else's image, as she silently vowed she would never enter that dark room.

Now it was time for the burning of the hazelnuts, and there was much laughter round the fireplace as Grannie told them what to do. "Shut your eyes and pick up two nuts, one in your right hand, one in your left. Next, place them on the fire and watch how they burn. If they burn together, it means he loves you and you will wed. If one jumps away, and that one bears the laddy's name, it means he cares not and will never be yours. Now, who will begin?"

Quick as lightning, Effie shut her eyes and snatched up two nuts, muttering under her breath, "right hand, Effie; left hand, Jimmie," and threw them into the coals. As soon as the one named Jimmie touched the fire, it bounded away in a shower of sparks, executed three or four leaps, and vanished up the chimney, leaving its companion to shrivel into a blackened husk.

A disappointed Effie tried to grab more nuts and when she was pulled back by her indignant companions, she cried out in passion, "It's no' fair! Ye could a' see there was something no' richt wi' thae nuts an' ah should get anither try!"

Jessie told her sharply, "The only thing wrong wi' them was that your lad could not get away from you quick enough! Try another name next year, Effie!"

And poor Effie had to watch the next pair burn steadily, side-by-side, with a fine blue light, to the applause of the onlookers.

Still simmering with resentment and disappointment, Effie forgot her fear of going into the dark-room, so determined was she to conjure up Jimmie's face.

The Love of Highland Mary

True to Grannie's instructions, she took a rosy apple in her right hand, a lighted candle in her left and stepped through the door which was promptly closed behind her. Trembling so hard that the candle cast jumping shadows, she peered into the mirror, gabbling out, "The lad whose face I wish to see, come to the glass and look at me." Biting large chunks from her apple, swallowing them whole and never taking her eyes from the mirror, Effie suddenly froze. Looking out at her was a huge face with flaming eyes and rows of awful teeth in a gaping red mouth. When that mouth spoke her name in a babbling wail, Effie came instantly out of her trance and throwing apple and candle any-which-way she rent the air with her howls as she burst through the door.

Mary caught her in her arms, but couldn't hold her, as Effie wrenched herself free and made for the one person who could save her from the Monster, old Grannie Urquhart. Reaching Grannie's chair, she flung herself before it, and buried her head in the old woman's lap. Gibbering with terror, she cried out, "Oh save me, Grannie! Save me from the Monster!"

Mary tried to raise her up, while Grannie Urquhart tut-tutted with annoyance, "Ye daft wee limmer that ye are! Ye've made me drop ma pipe and it's burnt a hole in ma best apron. Ah could skelp ye, that ah could!"

Burns came to help Mary lift Effie to her feet and Jessie held a glass of cold water to her mouth and forced her to drink it between wailing and coughing.

When they had quietened her sufficiently, Burns spoke soothingly. "Look, lassie, here's what you saw in the mirror." Effie stared at the turnip lantern, not burning now that the candle was out, and the reaction was too much for her. She burst into loud sobs of hysteria and, leaving the women to attend her, Burns and John Lees went off to seek out the one who had caused so much trouble. But here they had no luck and they guessed that the miscreant had long since fled.

"Just as well," Burns said grimly, "if I ever get my hands on him I'll give him a drumming he won't forget!"

"If only it hadn't been Effie," John groaned "Jessie, now, she'd have bashed him wi his own tumshie before he'd time to run!" Inside, things had settled down and bowls of hot sowens with butter melting on top, were handed round, with horn spoons to sup it. After this it was time for Grannie Urquhart to leave, and while her son fetched her shawls she beckoned Mary to her side, saying, "Bend down, lassie, and receive my blessing."

Looking at the wrinkled little face under the white mutch, Mary did as she was asked and felt the thistledown touch of the gnarled hand on her head. The old woman was quiet for a moment, and when she spoke her voice was so low that Mary had to lean close to hear it. "You will know great happiness, lassie. Hold to it while you can."

Turning to her son, she said wearily, "Tak' me hame, John, for it is woefu' I am, and sair at hert."

Tender as a woman, big John lifted his tiny Mother into his arms, soothing her with gentle words, and escorted by the others, carried her out to where the horse waited, and held her cradled against his breast, until she slept, and knew nothing of the long journey home. When Mary went to bed that night, she said a special prayer for the old woman who had promised her happiness and, since happiness to her meant Robert, Mary fell asleep smiling.

CHAPTER 14

Hogmanay 1785

On an early December day, Mary and Jessie set off to keep an appointment with Burns and Lees, their first meeting for more than three weeks, so unpredictable had been the weather with fogs, gales and rain.

As they approached the thorn tree, Jessie remarked, "You will not be sitting under there today, Mary. Look at it, dripping wet from every twig, and the seat soaking damp! Enough to give you the fever!"

Mary, sighing, could not argue, but brightened when Jessie said, "Never mind, lass, I'll walk on with John, and give you and Robert as much time together as I can."

When they saw the two men rounding the corner towards them, Jessie tugged at Mary's sleeve. "Don't forget to ask Robert about New Year. Tell him he and John are invited to join our Celebrations, and it would be a help to have some idea of numbers, as we will soon have to put up the puddings and the cakes."

When greetings had been exchanged, Jessie and John left the others to follow them to the bridge, and Robert, taking Mary's arm, slowed his steps to make sure they would not be overheard. Bending down to look into Mary's face, he said in a tone of held-in excitement, "Mary, what would you think if I asked you to leave Coilsfield?"

This unexpected question so startled Mary that she stopped walking to stare at Burns, asking in amazement, "Why, Robert? Why ever would you ask me to do such a thing?"

In his most persuasive voice, Burns went on to explain. "Well, lass, you know that I haven't been able to get over to see you during the bad weather, when the roads have been either flooded or blocked with snow?"

At Mary's nod of understanding, he went on. "Mrs Hamilton will have need of a nursemaid some time in February or March and she wishes to engage you as her nurse. She has been most impressed by what she has heard of you, and wants to meet you in order of offer the position. As Hamilton House is close to Mossgiel, we would be able to see one another oftener than we do now, and the extra money would mean more to send home. So, Mary, what do you say?"

For a moment, Mary said nothing, then drawing a deep breath, replied, "How can I answer, Robert, since it is not for me to make such a decision? You know that I am bound to Colonel and Mistress Montgomerie, and cannot leave without their consent. Also, there is my Father, who must decide what is best for me."

Seeing her troubled look, Burns drew her close, raising her face to his. "Of course, lassie, I understand. Mrs Hamilton will speak to Mrs Montgomerie, and Miss Campbell will write to your Father and ask for his permission, but only when you have met with Mrs Hamilton, and only if it is your wish to go to her, will a decision be taken."

All turned out as Robert said, and a meeting with Mrs Hamilton was arranged. A fine coach, with matching pair of chestnut horses, and resplendent coachman, was sent to take Mary and Robert to Hamilton Hall.

Mary sat back in the comfort of velvet-padded cushions and felt her feet sink into thick carpeting, while John, the coachman, handed Robert a rug to wrap around her knees, saying with a smile, "It's cold enough for snow, and Mistress Hamilton bade me look after the young lady."

Mary blushed under his admiring look, but Burns was not well pleased. He knew that the good-looking coachman had a way with the lassies and had no intention of allowing him to make advances to Mary. John met the warning frown on Rob's face with a mischievous wink as he mounted lithely to the driving seat, and with a crack of the whip he set the horses off at a brisk pace.

So well-sprung was the coach, it seemed to float over the ruts, and so well wrapped was Mary that she felt nothing of the cold wind which moved the bare trees to noisy rustlings against the grey sky. But most comforting of all was the warm clasp of Robert's hand on hers and his whispered compliments on her appearance. For him, she wore her blue bonnet, tied with broad silk ribbons in a bow under her chin, and her matching cloak, with its wide velvet collar, was simple of line and elegant.

"Are you nervous, Mary?" Burns asked.

Mary shook her head. "No, Robert, I do not think so. I may well feel a little uneasy when I am in front of Mrs Hamilton, but if you are beside me it will soon pass."

Burns squeezed her hand, "That's my good lassie," and at that moment the carriage came to a stop in front of a handsome, greystone mansion, with tall, narrow chimneys and wide, shallow steps leading up to a brass-studded door.

To the coachman's chagrin, Burns beat him by a hair's breadth to hand Mary down from the coach. Leading her up the steps, he lifted the metal rods on the door lintel and rattled them until suddenly the door was opened by a stately manservant in green livery. Once inside, they were divested of their cloaks and shown into a large drawing-room where a huge log fire blazed in a dancing glow of heat.

Mary recognised Gavin Hamilton, who hurried forward to greet them before turning to the woman who sat in a brocaded chair by the fire. With a hand under Mary's arm, he led her forward, saying in a loud, jovial voice, "Well, my dear, here is Robert's friend, Miss Campbell." Turning to Mary he said, "Miss Campbell, may I introduce you to my wife, who has been most anxious to meet you, as I have myself."

Mary felt the clasp of a soft, plump hand and looked down at Mrs Hamilton. She saw a flushed, pretty face with a rosebud mouth and round, hazel eyes, smiling up at her.

"Miss Campbell, I am delighted that you have come. Now do sit down so that we can have a talk." The voice, like a chime of wind-bells, went on "Gavin, my dear, take Robert into the Library while I get to know Miss Campbell."

Mary met Robert's questioning gaze and smiled in reassurance. She liked Mrs Hamilton, and felt no anxiety at being left alone with her. Isabella Hamilton, now in the sixth month of her pregnancy, was intrigued by the appearance of the young woman seated opposite her. She noted the innate poise, the air of quiet self-assurance and the unusual good looks. She liked the simple lines of her gown, the lack of ostentation lending it a refinement often lacking in the fashion of the times.

Skilled in assessing people, Mrs Hamilton drew from Mary her background, her work with children, her home and family, and thought the soft Highland lilt made her voice a very pleasant thing to listen to. This was another point in her favour, the purity of her English being much more pleasing to the ear than the Scots of the Lowlander.

Mrs Hamilton rang the bell for tea to be brought in and asked Mary to pour. She smiled approvingly at the deft handling of the china, the passing of sugar and cream, and the respectful way Mary held back until her hostess raised her cup.

"So, Miss Campbell, you have had experience of being in charge of infants from birth? Well, that is what I would like you to do here. My other children are older and have a Governess, and you would have a Nursery to yourself. I expect to have my Lying-in about the end of February, and if you agree to come to me, it would be best if you came at the beginning of that month."

Isabella Hamilton was now determined to have this girl as her baby's Nurse, and exerted her considerable powers of persuasion to this end, leaning forward to say, coaxingly, "Do, please, say you will accept."

Mary drew in her breath and steadily gave her answer, "I will be very happy to accept, Mistress Hamilton, if Mistress Montgomerie permits and if my Father gives his approval."

Satisfied, Isabella Hamilton looked at her and laughed rougishly, "And Robert, will he approve?"

Mary felt the colour rise in her cheeks, and was unable to meet Mrs Hamilton's eyes, but when Mr Hamilton and Robert joined them, there was no doubt that Burns was more than delighted to hear the news.

When Mary and Robert had taken their leave, Isabella Hamilton looked over at her husband as he stood with his back to the fire, hands clasped beneath his coat-tails. Tapping her cheek with her fan, she asked, "What did you think of Miss Campbell, Gavin?"

Her husband whistled softly between his teeth before he replied. "She is a very bonnie lass, not at all like Robert's usual lights-of-love. There is something sincere and modest in her demeanour, and I like the way she speaks. She's a cut above the servant lassies around these parts."

Mrs Hamilton nodded her satisfaction. "Exactly my own opinion! And did you see how they looked at each other? She smiled at him, and he knew at once that she had accepted the position. His whole face lit up, and that without a word being spoken."

Gavin Hamilton went over to embrace his pretty little wife, but his thoughts he kept to himself. He intended to see that Burns spent the next months putting together a collection of his poems and songs, enough for a book, and he didn't mean anything or anyone to distract him.

That night in the big, warm kitchen of Montgomerie House, there was consternation at the news of Mary's impending departure to the Hamilton Household. They were gathered round the supper table, everyone talking at once, while Mary sat silently listening and turning her head from one speaker to the other.

Jessie at last put an end to it, by bringing her pewter tankard down with such force that the ale spilled over and, her powerful voice raised to full pitch, overrode them all. "Hold your tongues, the lot of you! You're making noise enough to raise the roof, like a screechin' of hens with a fox in the hen-house!" She turned her scarlet face to Mary and, her voice gentled, asked, "Shall I tell them, Mary, or will you?"

Mary looked at her gratefully before replying, "If you would be so kind, Jessie. You will be better understood, see you."

Jessie nodded briskly. "Right then, here goes! Today, Mary was offered the position of Nursemaid to Mrs Hamilton, to be in charge of the new bairn that is expected in February next year." Jessie paused for a moment, holding up her hand as voices were raised. "I do not want to hear any questions till I am finished." Her gaze was stern enough to quell the hub-bub and she continued, "With the expectation of the full consent of Colonel and Mrs Montgomerie, and of Captain Campbell, Mary has accepted and will take up her new position at the end of January."

Effie burst into noisy tears, and sobbing bitterly, she ran to throw her arms round Mary's neck, pleading with her not to go. "Dinnae leave me, Mary. Och dinnae leave me."

Gently, Mary soothed her, wiping her wet face, while assuring her they would meet often. "Betty will go on helping you with your letters, won't you, Betty?"

Close to tears herself, Betty asked, "Why do you have to go, Mary? Are you not happy here?"

As the others put in their protests and pleas, Mary looked helplessly at the Cook, and Jessie, the one who would miss her most, had to swallow the lump in her throat before she could speak. "Wheest ye now, and stop jabberin' at the lassie! Mary has a very good reason for taking on her new job. Her Father oftimes cannot sail his boat to the Broomielaw to collect his coal and so has no cargoes for the islands. Mary will earn double her wages for being Nursemaid, and that will go to help out with the young ones at home."

This was something they could all understand, and it silenced their protests, but Effie buried her head on Mary's shoulder and would not be consoled.

Jessie knew how much Mary's calm, happy

disposition had contributed to the well-being of the kitchen, and how much she herself had come to depend on Mary's companionship. Shaking herself out of the doldrums, she poured an extra drink for each one, before setting them to think of tasks waiting to be done before the New Year.

"With Mary leaving, we're going to make this the best Hogmanay party ever! So, tomorrow we'll begin preparation. We'll start with shortbread, made with real butter, and I'll want all the moulds brought out and scrubbed."

"What about the Black Bun?" put in Jean. "For that, we'll have to crack the almonds, peel and blanch the nuts, and pick over the currants and raisins."

Jessie nodded. "Well, we've plenty of ingredients, including some of the Master's best brandy. And Mary, I'd like you to see to the pastry for the crust."

Jean's husband, Willie, put himself in charge of getting the bonfire ready, with Davie and Jimmie offering to gather stacks of dried branches and pine logs.

The days of preparation filled the kitchen with mouth-watering smells, of baking pies, plum puddings, cakes and buns. Finally, the turkeys, geese and fowls were stuffed and placed ready for the ovens. Green, aromatic fir branches decorated the doors and walls, along with red holly-berries in their dark green leaves.

Jessie looked, and was satisfied. An exclamation from Mary startled her out of her reverie, and she asked sharply, "Guid sakes, lassie, what ails you?"

"Look!" Mary pointed to the window.

Jessie gasped, "Snow! The very night before Hogmanay!" She joined Mary at the window and, peering out, said hopefully, "Maybe it's just a passing flurry and won't last long."

But as they watched, the white flakes drifted faster and faster from a leaden grey sky and a wind got up to pelt them against the window panes where they soon blotted out the light.

For a moment, the two women were silent, each busy with her own thoughts. Mary knew that if the blizzard continued, the roads would be blocked off, making it impossible for anyone to get through. A bitter pang of disappointment gripped her as she thought of Robert. He had promised to be with her to usher in the New Year, before returning to his family at Mossgiel, and she knew it would all be meaningless without his presence.

Jessie thought of John Lees, his merry, joking face alight with laughter, his hand on her neck as he tried to snatch a kiss, his whispered, "Ach, Jessie, it's a heart of stone is in your breast."

She had planned to show him differently at the sound of the midnight bells, but now it looked as if she wouldn't get the chance.

Jessie and Mary were brought out of their silence by rushing feet and excited voices, as Effie and Jimmie stampeded into the kitchen, closely followed by Jean and Betty. Effie couldn't contain herself and gasped out, "Mary, Jessie, we're goin' to have a white New Year! It's snawin' an' blawin' and the men are fair swearin' an awfu' lot o' bad words."

Jimmie, his squint seeming worse than ever, sniggered, "Dod aye! Some swear words I've never heard before frae auld Willie!" This so angered Jean that she hit him a buffet on the ear, with a warning to mind his manners before she pushed him out the door to help the men put canvas covers over the bonfire, to protect it from the snow.

Next morning, Mary awoke to an eerie silence. The room seemed to float in a shadowy white light and she instinctively looked at the window, to find it had disappeared.

Shivering in the icy air, she sat up, and rubbing her eyes, saw that snow covered each window-pane. She heard Betty stir, and her sleepy voice complain, "I'm freezing, Mary. It can't be time to get up!"

But it was, and throwing on their clothes they fled to the head of the kitchen, where the fire had been banked up and now was poked vigorously by Jessie into leaping red flames.

Soon, the men joined them, stamping and scraping their boots to knock off the snow, clapping their arms to restore circulation, and blowing on frozen fingers before grasping mugs of hot tea.

Mary couldn't wait to ask anxiously, "What are the roads now like? And is the snow finished, think you?"

The men shook their heads doubtfully. "The winds have caused drifts that cover the hedges, and the road is many feet under. But the sky is brighter, and we've maybe seen the worst of it."

With that, Mary had to be content, and when she ventured out into the garden, she had to shade her eyes against the dazzling white light. As the day wore on, hope rose in her heart that somehow, Robert would find a way to come to her. Silently, wordlessly, she sent her thoughts to him, and was sure she felt his love reach out to reassure her.

By nine that night, a full moon lit the snow-capped trees, the blanketed hedges, the frozen grasses, to a silvered prism of rainbow lights that sparkled against the eyes. Inside, the fire burned and leapt and the pots and kettles bubbled quietly on the hot-plates, emitting clouds of fragrant steam. The long table was set ready with plates, bowls and tankards, a sprig of red holly-berries beside each place. Ranged on the serving shelves were the cakes and puddings, the pies and sweetmeats, to follow the roast turkeys and fowl. Would their guests brave the snow-covered roads, was the question everyone asked and none could answer.

Suddenly, a jangling of bells and a loud "hurroo!" startled them to their feet, and in the rush to the door, Mary beat the others to be first, with Jessie close on her heels. Looking out, they saw a conveyance built on wide runners, drawn by a grey mare with bells on the harness. Driving it was the caped, muffled figure of Robert Burns, with John Lees at his side. They were followed by other sledges, but Mary had eyes only for Robert, whose high spirits set a light to her own. He jumped down, pulled the scarf away from his face, and swept her indoors, leaving the men to stable the horse.

That night the atmosphere in the kitchen was one of rollicking good cheer, but Mary never remembered what she ate, so great was her happiness that her prayers had been answered. She ate the choice pieces of turkey he served to her, and drank the wine he poured into her glass, but far more than food and drink was his presence at her side.

Ten minutes before the hour of twelve, the tables were cleared and everyone gathered outside to hear the midnight bells. Willie the gardener held a lighted pitch torch, the piper warmed up his bagpipes, and then, as the first stroke of the Church bell rang out, a silence fell until the last chime faded. Then, a great shout rent the air, the torch was thrust into the bonfire and the pipes swelled in a rousing march. Cries of a "Guid New Year" resounded, and Mary, enfolded in Robert's arms, wished him in the Gaelic, "Slainte, sonas agus beartas" (Health, wealth and happiness) and in return received his kiss and his blessing, "May the year 1785 bring you all that your heart desires, my dearest lass. God bless you."

And so began for Mary a new year and a new beginning, the year of seventeen hundred and eighty five.

CHAPTER 15

Hamilton Hall

At the end of January, Mary arrived at Hamilton Hall. The mistress of the house was there to greet her in person, and welcomed her warmly. With only a month left before her lying-in, Isabella Hamilton was heavy with child, but concealed it well beneath her layered silk gown. She introduced Mary to her eight year old daughter, Agnes, and her ten year old son, John, whose Governess, a thin, acidulated figure dressed in black, offered a less than cordial, "Good morning."

The children studied Mary with lively interest, wondering why she did not speak in Gaelic, for they had been told she was a Highlander. They made up their minds to find out, the moment they got her on her own, well knowing what their Governess would say if they broke her strict rule that "children should be seen and not heard".

The Governess, Miss Lismore, had her own ideas about the new Nursemaid. She dubbed her too good-looking, too tall, and altogether too much above herself! Sourly, she considered the way Mrs Hamilton fussed over her as encouraging this idea, and bridled when she was told to show Miss Campbell to her sleeping-quarters in the Nursery.

She led the way upstairs, and Mary following, noted the outrage in the ramrod-stiff back, and wisely kept silent.

When she saw the large, bright room with windows overlooking gardens still white with frost, and a glowing fire lighting up the walls, Mary exclaimed with pleasure, "But how fine is the room, and happy it will be for the new child."

Miss Lismore made no response, except to open a door and point out the bed it contained, together with a clothes-stand and a table with a finely decorated jug and basin. "This is where you will sleep, and hot water will be brought to you each morning."

Before Mary could reply, the scuffling figures of John and Agnes Hamilton erupted into the room, with John in the lead. His first words were to ask to hear Mary speak in the Gaelic, and hiding her amusement, she answered him.

Miss Lismore was outraged. Grabbing John by the ear, she exploded, "How dare you break into Miss Campbell's room like a common peasant! Leading your sister into mischief as usual. Your Father will hear of this, I promise you!"

John yelped in pain, but still begged Mary to tell him what she had said.

Mary turned to the Governess. "Miss Lismore, your pardon I beg for my rudeness in using the Gaelic. If you permit me, I will this time say the words in the English."

Not for a moment would the Governess have asked this on her own, but her curiosity piqued, Mary's apology gave her the opportunity she wished for. Stiffly she replied, "Very well, Miss Campbell, you have my permission" at the same time letting go of John's ear to his audible relief.

Mary repeated, in English, "My goodness, young man, you sound just like my brother Robert, when he was your age! We called him 'Rab the Pirate'."

When the children heard this, Agnes's eyes became as round as saucers, while John's glittered with excitement. Forestalling his questions, Mary addressed his Governess. "I hope my speech gives no offence, Miss Lismore, for indeed none was so intended."

She sensed a softening in that lady's manner, as she believed Mary's words to be a reprimand to her impetuous pupil, and was prepared to accept it as such.

John's burning desire to learn more about 'Rab the Pirate' was frustrated as he and his sister were sternly removed from the Nursery, but he promised himself to find out more about him at the first opportunity.

In the days that followed, Mary settled into a very different way of life at Hamilton Hall. Her time was spent mostly on sewing small garments for the expected infant, and neatly hemming fine cotton squares for sheets and napkins.

Her meals were brought to her in the Nursery, by one of the kitchen-maids, who later removed them with a respectful curtsey and a few murmered words. This isolation from the other members of staff gave Mary a feeling of loneliness she had never experienced before, and she did not enjoy it. But she knew better than to intrude into the kitchen, where her presence would cause resentment and unease.

When Mrs Hamilton came to inspect Mary's work, she was deeply appreciative of the fine stitching and the clever design of the several items already completed. She picked up a cream flannel gown, ruched and smocked in silk thread, and said admiringly, "Why, Mary, what truly beautiful work! Where did you learn to sew like this?"

Mary told her quietly, "I learned it from my Mother, when I was quite young. I used to watch her when she would be making clothes for me and my brother, and later I helped make baby things for my little sister, Agnes, and my brother Archibald."

Isabella Hamilton had another reason for her visit, one which, she knew, would bring much pleasure to Mary. Carefully replacing the robe, she said, "I have some good news, Mary, good news for both of us. Mr Hamilton has just returned from Glasgow, and with him is your friend, Mr Burns."

Watching the girl's expressive face, she saw the blue eyes light up like stars, and a vivid blush stain her cheeks carnation pink.

Mrs Hamilton smiled, well-pleased at Mary's obvious delight, "Yes. I thought that would make you happy. Now I will take you to the Drawing room where a certain young man is waiting to see you."

Mary remembered little of the walk downstairs and along the corridors, except the slowness of it as Mrs Hamilton leaned heavily on her arm.

But she did not forget the sight of Robert as the great, carved doors opened to show him facing towards her. It was as though she were seeing him for the first time, tall, broad-shouldered, black hair framing his handsome face, brown eyes shining in welcome.

Hands outstretched, he came to her, and wordlessly, his eyes looked deep into hers. Still gazing into her face, he took her hands in his and raised them to his lips and heard her whisper his name, "Robert".

His firm mouth curved in a smile, but all he said was her own name, "Mary".

Gavin Hamilton, his arm around his little wife, now claimed their attention. "Good day to you, Miss Mary," he said, "and it is happy we are to be back from Glasgow. As Robert will tell you, there are many of our friends wishful to hear more of his poems and songs, and already plans are afoot to have our Rob's work printed in a book! What think you of that?"

Before Mary could answer, Mrs Hamilton spoke quickly, "My dear, do give Mary time to catch her breath before she passes an opinion, and let Robert himself tell her about it." Firmly, she urged him from the room, determined to give Mary and Robert a few precious moments together.

When they left, Burns shook his head, a frown creasing his forehead as he looked at Mary's face. "Gavin shouldn't have blurted it out like he did. I wanted to break the news to you myself."

Mary touched his hand and smiled at him. "It is of no matter, my dear. Surely it is very wonderful for you, and a thing you have long desired."

Her words chased the cloud from his face, and words poured from him. "You are the only one who understands me, Mary, and understands all that this could mean to me. It is the key to a new life, an end to the drudgery of ploughing and farming, with never time to take my ease. But see you, lassie, it means spending all my spare time writing down my songs and putting my bits of poetry onto paper. It will take more than a few ideas to make a book, but I can and I will do it, no matter how long it takes, if you will stay by me."

Looking at him, Mary did not doubt his determination, nor his ability to succeed, and unhesitatingly she gave him her promise.

In the small morning-room, Gavin Hamilton was laying his own plans for his gifted protégé. He broached the subject of his wife's confinement, asking if everything was ready for the birth of the child, and was assured that Doctor and Nurse would take up residence on the due date. Now he said, "That is good, my dear, and I have a treat in store for you when you have quite recovered from it all."

Isabella raised her eyebrows at this, asking, "What do you mean, Gavin? What sort of treat?"

Her husband looked at her. "Well, I was not going to say anything about it until the infant was here, but I believe it will help you through your travail, if you know what is planned. I have arranged for you to travel to Edinburgh to holiday with your parents, taking the child and Mary with you. You are to stay as long as it takes to recover your health, with no household chores to upset you. So, what do you think of my idea, sweeting?"

Isabella Hamilton, by no means an intellectual, was nonetheless not a stupid woman, and she sensed something behind her husband's offer which puzzled her. Shaking her head to rid it of an idea that lurked beyond her grasp, she gave way to anticipation. She hated and feared the pains of labour, and knew that her husband was right. Just to think of relaxing under her parents loving care would help to take her mind off the birth. So now she said, truthfully, "I like your idea very much, husband, and if you contrive to visit us in the Capital that will make it quite perfect."

Gavin Hamilton was satisfied. With Mary out of the way in Edinburgh, he would see to it that Burns concentrated all his energies on his writing. His own conviction of Burns' genius had been confirmed by the reaction of his friends in Glasgow, when they listened to the young farmer read his poems. Gavin Hamilton knew it would be a feather in his cap to be the patron of such a poet, and the publication of his book would set Burns on the road to fame and fortune.

When, at the end of February, Isabella Hamilton gave birth to a son, christened Alexander, the scene was set for change. Three weeks later, Mrs. Hamilton, her Maid, Mary and the baby, together with his Wet-nurse, were on their way to the city of Edinburgh.

CHAPTER 16
Jean Armour

O
n her first morning in Charlotte Square, Mary awoke to the cries of the vendors and the noisy clatter of horses and wheels on the paved, cobblestoned streets.

Still half-asleep, she found herself unable to adjust to the strangeness of the room. Through the tall, narrow window the sun cast dancing gleams of light, and slowly, she picked out the cradle in the corner, and the open door of the room where the Wet-nurse slept.

Bit-by-bit, she remembered their arrival in the Square, and the warmth of the welcome given to Mrs Hamilton by her parents, as she all but tumbled out of the coach into their waiting arms. Her bonnet crooked, her face flushed with happiness, Isabella Hamilton turned to take her new son from Mary and present him to his Grandparents.

After that, she recalled the square, spacious hall, full of light from tall, stained-glass windows, an elegant, curved staircase, and many panelled doors. She had been shown into the Housekeeper's sitting-room, and served tea and cakes at a little, oval table, where a silver teapot steamed gently.

Fully awake now, Mary remembered the House-keeper's name, Mrs Forbes, a name which suited the plump figure, with face, bosom and hips all as round as cottage-loaves. Altogether, Mary had found the Housekeeper's presence comforting, and had enjoyed talking to her.

In the days that followed, with doting Grandparents and an army of servants all clamouring to look after the baby, Mary found herself with a great deal of free time on her hands. She would have preferred to explore the city on her own, but was sent out, by Mrs Anderson's orders, in a smart carriage, whose driver was instructed to take her wherever she wanted to go.

Her first excursion, on Mrs Anderson's advice, was a visit to the Castle. The carriage left the elegant houses in Charlotte Square to bowl along streets which grew narrower and darker, with the tall tenements shutting out the sky. James, the coachman, pointed his whip and said, "Well, Miss Campbell, look up the cliff and ye'll see the auld Castle."

Mary felt a shiver go through her as she looked up at the sheer rock on which was perched the grey, grim fortress that was the Castle. She was glad of James' company as they walked through the gates into the courtyard, and climbed up to the ramparts. There, they were met by the noise of many soldiers, stamping, marching, wheeling, to the stentorian voice of the Sergeant.

In complete contrast was the peace of Queen Margaret's Chapel, dim and cool after the glare of the outside world.

Refreshed, Mary visited the small, wood-panelled room where Mary, Queen of Scots, had given birth to a son, a Prince of Scotland.

The passionate words uttered by Robert Burns were clear in her mind, "Aye, he was born to silk sheets and satin robes, this bairn who was our King James the Sixth of Scotland and First of England. But when the English Elizabeth died and named him her successor, he couldn't wait to shake the dust of Scotland from his feet. Off he galloped, to have his boots licked by the English, and came back once only to his native land."

Mary heard again the biting scorn of his voice as he expressed his contempt for a King who deserted his country for a "mess of potage".

As Mary explored the city of Edinburgh, she found much to admire, but the streets, the noise, the smoke, wearied her, and she longed for the green fields and the soft breezes of Ayrshire. She admitted to herself that of all the things she missed, the voice, the presence, of Robert Burns were the deepest felt.

Soon after, the warm sunshine of early April was swept away in a tearing East wind of hail and sleet. Mary could barely make out the gardens of the Square and knew that little would be left of the daffodils and tulips, come quick to bloom in the sun's heat and as quick to die in the wintry blasts which felled them.

Roaring fires were lit in every room, and as the hail rattled against the windows, Mary sat down to write to Robert. She wrote, haltingly, of the things she had seen, the Castle, the Queen's room, the street called the Royal Mile which led to the Palace of Holyrood and its Abbey, now only a derelict ruin.

Staring at the fire, seeing pictures in the flames, Mary wrote on. "A thing has surprised me greatly, that here are many Highland men and women, so that I hear my own tongue spoken everywhere, and a great pleasure it is to me." Pausing, Mary sorted out in her mind the things she knew Robert would like to know and, with doubts over her spelling, wrote on, "This day, it is not April. See out of the window I cannot. The sleet is over all the glass and flowers are flat, flat under white, cold snow and the sound in the fire is the Water Kelpie, screaming, howling wild in Fury". She ended her letter with a simple salutation, "To Robert Burns from Mary Campbell". She folded the paper over, tucked the ends in, and addressed it to "Mr R Burns, Mossgiel" to be given into the hands of Mr Hamilton, who had arrived that morning from Carlisle.

On his return from Kilmarnock, Burns' first call was to Hamilton Hall, to see Mary. Filled with anticipation, he whistled gaily as he rattled the iron rod hanging by the side of the door. The little servant who opened up to him bobbed a curtsey and drew aside to let him in. The silence in the hall was noticeable, and Burns, looking round, was puzzled. "Is Mr. Hamilton not at home, lass?"

Nervously, the maid stammered out, "No, sir, nor nobody else," then, with relief, fled to the kitchen as the Housekeeper appeared. Mrs Smith, apologising for the way he had been greeted, took him into the Drawing room.

Sitting opposite him, she began without dissembly. "Everyone is away to Edinburgh, to Mrs Hamilton's parents. Mr. Hamilton has been in Carlisle and should by now have joined his wife. He left word for you, that he would be home next week."

Burns thought this over, and then asked, "And the others, when do they return?" Mrs Smith shook her head. "That I cannot say, but I hope it will be soon, for I miss Mary's company more than I can tell. The place just isn't the same without her, singing lullabies to the bairn, coming to my room to drink tea and telling me stories about Campbeltown."

This was too much for Burns, bringing to mind his own need for Mary. Quickly, he rose to his feet and took his leave of Mrs Smith. It was as well for Burns that his horse knew the road to Mossgiel without necessity for touch or speech, as, lost in his thoughts, he forgot everything else.

His thoughts were not happy. There had not even been a letter from Mary, and a verbal message only from Hamilton. The empty house had seemed to him a bad omen, and he felt himself deserted. He had no illusions about his weakness, and knew that his quick passions could well lead him into a dalliance with the first willing lass to cross his path, a thing he had not indulged in since knowing Mary. And, he sensed, a thing that now would bring him little pleasure, only remorse.

That night, accompanied by his brother, Gilbert, Burns sought the solace of Poosie Nancy's Inn. The April night was warm, and the door to the Inn stood open, to let out the clouds of wood-smoke that billowed from each ingle-nook fire. The smell of beer and wine, the din of drunken voices and drunker songs bellowed out with force, if not with melody, assailed their ears as the brothers entered.

Draining his tankard of ale, Burns noted Jockie, the old soldier, his doxie nodding in his grasp, as they supped their whisky and loudly kissed. His loneliness eased by the convivial atmosphere, Burns pointed out to Gilbert the red rags of a once proud uniform, and the fact that old Jock had given a leg and an arm for his country, "and all he's gained is a Beggar's badge."

Then, as the old soldier staggered up, a burst of applause encouraged him to sing a marching song, accompanied by raucous laughter from his doxie and the banging of mugs on tables.

Gilbert shouted in Robert's ear, "Well, by heavens, it hasnae broken his spirit! Look at him jump, and thump his wooden leg!"

As the brothers made their unsteady way home, the coolness of the night breeze played over their heated brows and Burns lifted his face gratefully to the sky. He saw the stars shining fitfully down upon him, and their clean, pure, light reminded him of Mary. He spoke her name under his breath. "Mary, my bonnie lass, you are the bright Pole-star I set my compass by. Come you home soon and keep me hand-fast by your side".

In Edinburgh, Mary sat by the window, thinking of Robert. The stars were beginning to shine in the pale evening sky, and to them Mary addressed her thoughts. "Robert, I am wishing to be with you under the stars this night. Once, you said the same stars shine down on us, wherever we are, and that comforts me. Know you, that you are my last thought at night and my first thought in the morning and never do I forget to 'say-you' in my prayers."

When Gavin Hamilton took leave of his wife and prepared to set off for Ayrshire, he assured Mary that her letter would be given into Robert's hands as soon as he reached Mauchline. Seeing her wistful look and guessing rightly the cause of it, he patted her shoulder and told her, "You'll be seeing Robert yourself, lass, in a few week's time, and the pair of you will have plenty to tell each other, I daresay."

Mary blushed so prettily that Hamilton envied his friend, and almost regretted that he had been the means of separating them. He had to remind himself that he had their best interests at heart, and that they would thank him for it one day. Success as a poet could well be in reach of Burns within a year, bringing with it fame and rich rewards.

And who, he now asked himself, was best fitted to

be at Robert's side? His early doubts forgotten, he acknowledged that Mary Campbell was the one that he would choose. Bonnie in looks, quietly dignified, possessed of a sound good sense, she could well prove to be the calming influence needed to balance Burns' mercurial nature.

Mary's thoughts were with Hamilton every mile of the way to Ayrshire. She pictured him handing the letter to Robert, the glow in his brown eyes when he saw her writing, and how eagerly he would hurry off to read it in private. Though Mary did not know it, the truth was far otherwise.

Gavin Hamilton did not see Burns for some days after his return. Business kept him at his Glasgow office, but when he at last reached Hamilton Hall, he lost no time in sending a message to invite Burns to dine.

At six o'clock that evening, Burns walked into the Drawing-room of his friend who asked for his news. "But first, I have been charged by a certain young lady to put this into your hands."

Anticipating Burns warm pleasure to receive the letter, Hamilton was totally surprised at his reaction. Looking at Mary's handwriting, he uttered a sound so despairing it shook Gavin Hamilton to the core. At the same time a ghostly pallor spread over his face.

"Speak up, Robert," Hamilton demanded, "for surely nothing can be so bad as your countenance proclaims?"

His words fell on deaf ears. Burns sat like one turned to stone, until he raised his eyes to his friend and said, in a travesty of his usual voice; "Bad? Aye, there's bad and worse than bad, and nothing to be done about it! Nothing!"

He laid Mary's letter on the table, and smoothing it

under his hand, he went on in a dull monotone, "When I got back from Kilmarnock and found Mary had gone, I was in despair. That night, I went to Nancy's Inn, and had a bit too much to drink, but went no further than that. It was the next night brought about my ruination."

Here his voice failed him, and he sat lost in a trance of misery so deep that Hamilton was driven to shake him almost violently to get him to continue his story. Burns went on, "It was the night of the Ayr Races, and to pass the time, I went with Gilbert to the Dance. It was the first dance I'd been at since I met Mary, and what with missing her, needing her, I went clean daft! Right out of my wits I was, what with the drink, the music and the reels. The upshot of it all is, that I paired off with a lass and I've promised to marry her."

Gavin Hamilton felt light-headed with relief as he slapped Burns on the back. "Man, Robert, that's easy recanted! Give the lass a gold piece and she'll be well enough pleased, I'll warrant."

Burns shook his head, "You don't understand, Gavin. This is no servant lass, like Lizzie. She's one of the Mauchline Beauties. It's wee Jean Armour."

For once in his life, Gavin Hamilton was struck dumb. After a minute, he cleared his throat to ask in disbelief, "Are you telling me she's the daughter of old Armour, the Master Mason?"

Burns sighed and groaned in the same breath. "Aye, that's right, and since we've known each other, she's terrified out of her wits there might be a bairn, and so I've given her a Marriage paper in case her Father ever finds out."

Now the lawyer in Hamilton took over. "Does anyone else know about this?" Burns shook his head. "No, nor likely to. Jean isn't about to let her shame be known."

"Well, then, if there's to be no outcome, the paper can be torn up."

Burns looked at him. "No, it cannot! Jean has it fast, and I have lost the most precious thing in my life, I have lost Mary."

Hamilton realising the part he had played in all this, had a feeling of troubles to come. Jean Armour's Father was a proud man, and never would consent to his daughter marrying Robert Burns, whose reputation as a womaniser and, worse, a mocker of the Church, was known throughout the County.

Burns bowed his head, to rest his face on Mary's letter, and said, "Do you know the words in the Bible, about 'the abomination of desolation'? Well, it is all around me, right this minute, with none to blame but myself, though I swear I never meant it to happen."

Shortly after, he took his leave, saying, with a new hardness in his voice, "Never fear, Gavin, you'll have your book yet. It's money I'll need to sweeten old Armour and help me support a wife. Jean's a bonny enough lass, though a timid one, and I'll stand by her, but the wife I dreamt of having was always Mary."

"Will you write to her, Robert?"

"No, that is the coward's way out. I will call on her when she returns, if only to say goodbye."

"But she will understand, and forgive you. I'm sure of that."

"Aye, that she will, from the goodness of her heart, but I will never forgive myself! Through my damned infernal weakness, I've lost her, and now I must bide with the Devil and sup his bitter brew!"

CHAPTER 17

The Bastard Wean

By the end of May, Hamilton Hall was fully occupied once more. The familiar surroundings of the Nursery brought a measure of comfort to Mary, as did the feel of the baby's soft body as she cradled him in her arms, soothing him with tender Gaelic lullabies. But the joy she had anticipated at being reunited with Robert, had turned to ashes.

She remembered that moment in Edinburgh when Mrs Hamilton had sent for her. Thinking it was something to do with the coming journey, she had been totally unprepared for employer's words, although the seriousness of Isabella's pretty face had somewhat puzzled her, as had her voice when she told her to sit down.

"Mary, there is something I have to tell you, about Robert."

At this, Mary was seized by a feeling of dread and whispered, "Robert? He is ill? Or . . . or . . . ?" She could not finish the terrible thought.

At the striken look on the girl's face, Mrs Hamilton cried out, "No, No, Mary, my dear, it is not that. Indeed, it is something quite otherwise!"

The relief to Mary was so great that she was hardly aware of what followed, and obediently sipped the wine which Mrs Hamilton poured for her. She heard, as one in a daze, that Robert was promised in Marriage to someone he had newly met, according to Mrs Hamilton. Hearing this, a light went out in Mary's life.

Seeing the quenched look on her face, Isabella Hamilton cried out in anger, "How could he do this to you? It is a dishonourable act, and I shall tell him so!"

But Mary held up her hands, palms outwards, and a spark of life came back to her eyes as she said, quietly but firmly, "No, Robert is not dishonourable. He promised nothing to me, and is free to do as he wishes." Here Mary's voice faltered, and she could not go on. She could remember little of the next two days that followed. Preparation to leave Edinburgh occupied all her time, and left her so wearied at night that she slept without dreams.

As she laid the now sleeping babe in his cradle, a knock on the door heralded the arrival of one of the maids, with a message from Mrs Hamilton that Mary was wanted in the Drawing-room. Quickly, Mary smoothed her hair, with a brief glance in the mirror to check on any stray tendrils. She straightened the white muslin fichu which set off the new summer dress, one of three which her employer had ordered for her in Edinburgh. The deep blue cotton matched her eyes. But Mary gave no thought to her appearance; it was enough that she was neat and tidy, and that the dress was light and cool in the warmth of the early June heatwave.

Tapping gently on the door, Mary walked in, expecting to find Mrs Hamilton waiting for her. Nothing had prepared her for the sight of Robert Burns, and she gave a little, inarticulate cry as she reached to grasp the door-handle for support.

Burns took one step towards her, then stopped, his hands outstretched, his anguished gaze fixed on her white face, as he stammered, "Mary, lass, I didn't mean to come on you so suddenly . . . but I thought if you knew I was here, you would have refused to see me."

Mary looked at him, and with a great throb of pity, she realised that here was a Robert she had never seen before, his whole bearing that of a man unsure of himself, and unsure of his reception. More, she sensed his desperate unhappiness, and in a sudden need to dispel it, she said quickly, "No, Robert, that never would I have done! I have been told you are to marry, but that is all. And you need not feel you must tell me more. I have told Mrs Hamilton there is no dishonour on your part, that we have ever been true friends, and that though things must now be different, yet I will remain always your friend."

The sincerity of Mary's words, her steadfast defence of his honour, added to the remorse Burns felt, and he had to turn away to hide the quick tears which threatened to unman him.

The arrival of a maid, with glasses and a decanter of wine, helped him to master his emotions, until he saw Mary move to open the door which the maid had closed. That one act brought home to him, as nothing else could have done, the finality of his relationship with this dearest of companions. Sore at heart, he waited until Mary was seated at the table, before offering her a glass of wine, which she accepted, but barely touched with her lips. Sorrowfully, she watched him drain his own glass in one swift movement, and fill it again with an unsteady hand. This time, he made no attempt to drink, but sat gazing into the ruby depths. Mary waited, longing to reach out to him, but knowing well that this time she could not ease his pain.

At last, a deep, shuddering sigh escaped from Burns' lips, and he lifted his head to meet Mary's eyes in a silent communion. In his gaze, she read his remorse, his agonised plea for understanding and forgiveness. Hers mutely offered him all he asked for, with the promise of an unshakable trust. For a long moment, mind spoke to mind, until spontaneously, their hands met and held in a warm, firm grasp. When it ended, Mary stood up and spoke his name in the Gaelic, "Raibeart, know you that I will never cease to 'say-you' in my prayers."

And with that, she was gone. From the room, from his life.

Lost in thought, Burns unconsciously raised the glass of wine to his lips, then slowly and carefully, he set it down again, untouched. He did not need it. It was enough to know that Mary had not cast him out, was still his friend.

Neither Gavin Hamilton nor his wife, ever found out what, exactly, had passed between Mary and Burns, and life to all appearances, returned to normal at Hamilton Hall.

On her free afternoon, Mary set out to visit Jessie Smith at Montgomerie House. She enjoyed the cool breeze which set clouds flying across the blue sky, and the warm scent of the little pink and white briar roses was sweet on the air. Crossing the bridge over the Faile, Mary saw the water was a mere trickle after the drought of the past weeks, and she thought of autumn and winter when it overflowed its banks or was frozen hard under winter ice. Soon she arrived at the thorn tree, smothered now with thick, creamy white flowers, and, unable to resist, she sat down beneath the drooping branches and breathed in the intoxicating perfume of the hawthorn blossoms.

Eyes closed, mind drugged with the all-enveloping scent, memories crowded in on Mary. Her first tryst here with Robert, so vivid, she could see his face, brown eyes alight, firm lips smiling at her. She felt again the warm clasp of his fingers as he held her hand, heard the deep tones of his voice as he spoke her name, "Mary".

Like one coming out of a dream, Mary opened her eyes, to hear again her name being called, not in Robert's voice, but by Jessie Smith, crying from the path, asking, "Mary, is that you, or am I dreaming?"

Quickly, not wanting Jessie to join her under the tree, Mary rose and went to meet her friend. Jessie's keen eyes surveyed Mary's face with some anxiety, dreading to see unhappiness there. To her relief, there was none. Mary was as she remembered her, smiling and greeting her with unusual warmth as she said, "Jessie, it is glad I am to see you after so long an absence. Is all well with you?"

"Aye, Mary, well enough, I thank you. I thought we could talk easier out of the house, so come along with you and let's take a daunder." Arm-in-arm, they made their way along the grassy banks between masses of bluebells and foaming white spirea, half hidden by thick, green ferns. Without preamble, Jessie spoke out "I suppose you've heard the news of Robert? Of his courting of young Jean Armour?"

Quietly, Mary answered, "Yes, Mrs Hamilton told me in Edinburgh, and Robert called to tell me himself, two days ago, but the name was not mentioned."

Jessie's wrath broke forth at this. "I wonder he had the effrontery to face you, scoundrel that he is, to treat you so ill! Other lassies he has used lightly, but they've been no better that they should be, not like you."

Mary stopped and looked straight at her friend, with an expression Jessie had never seen before. "You must not miscall Robert, Jessie. He was not bound to me, and so was free to do as he wished. We are friends and always will be, although of course we cannot meet as once we did. His duty now lies with another. But he is no scoundrel."

Jessie was not appeased, and her reply was not conciliatory. "There are those who think otherwise, friends who are of my opinion."

Mary's look and voice, were stern. "They cannot be friends of mine." She added in softer tones, "But you, dear Jessie, are my best of friends after Robert, and if you show him no blame, speak him no ill, others will listen to you."

Unable to resist, Jessie took Mary in her arms and held her close, while she said with feeling, "Mary Campbell, you're either a Saint, or soft in the head! But if that's what you want of me, you shall have it." Moved out of her natural reserve, Mary bestowed a kiss on Jessie's poppy-red cheek, and held tightly to her arm as they walked on.

Jessie had another bit of news. "Robert's daughter is to be brought up by Mrs Burns at Mossgiel. They've called her Bess, and Lizzie Paton has gone off with a nice tocher to marry a milkman on a Border farm."

Colour rushed to Mary's cheeks, and she thought how joyful it would be to Mother Robert's child. Pain followed, as she reminded herself that this favour was not for her, but for the one to whom Robert had promised Marriage.

As they walked on, Jessie remarked, "That Lizzie has no morals whatever, to up and leave her babe with never a backward look. At least Robert acted the better part by providing for her future, and by keeping the infant beside him."

In a low voice, Mary said, "Have I not told you that Robert is no scoundrel, and hasn't he proved it, standing by the young woman and never denying the child is his?"

Jessie answered thoughtfully, "True, Mary, fair's fair, and no use saying other, but I doubt he'll no be so easy let-off with Miss Jean Armour. Her Father is a big man hereabouts and Jean's the apple of his eye. He'll not take kindly to her going with Robert, if ever he gets wind of it. He considers Rob to be ungodly, a womaniser and a blasphemer with no money and no prospects, and hasnae been blate in voicing his opinions, according to John Lees."

Mary looked troubled, thinking that such a proud, unbending man would rouse the very worst in Robert, whose own fiery nature would brook no such criticism. It did not bode well for the future.

The long, sunny days lasted all though June and July, and Mary busied herself in stitching new clothes for young Alexander. It gave her pleasure to see how fast he was growing as he kicked and gurgled under the shade of the chestnut tree.

She saw little of Robert these days, and knew of his movements only at second-hand. Just last night, Gavin Hamilton had entertained some friends to Supper, and from the half-open door, Mary had heard mention of Burns, as someone remarked loudly "Well, Hamilton, you must be feeling gey pleased with yourself. Your young farmer protégé, Burns, is attracting a lot of attention with his poems. I heard tell he can get as much as five shillings for half-a-dozen lines, and a guinea for a bawdy piece!"

Gavin Hamilton's voice, sounding displeased, answered, "Rumour is not always to be trusted, and from now on, all his writings are to be kept for his book."

From Jessie Smith, she learned that Robert was hardly ever at home. She told Mary of his invitations to the great houses of Lords and Lairds, all anxious to hear him read his poems, and added, with a sidelong glance at Mary's face, "It seems he'd rather be anywhere else than stay at home."

A stillness came over Mary as she pondered Jessie's words. Was there no happiness now for Robert at Mossgiel? Or was he so driven by the need to succeed that all else had to be set aside?

Knowing what was happening to Burns through her husband, Isabella Hamilton's sympathies were all for Mary. When she had learned of his 'Paper Marriage' to Jean Armour, she was provoked to exclaim, "Is there no end to this young man's foolishness! For all his brains and book-learning, his talents as a writer, he shows no common-sense whatever when it comes to muddling up his life. A Marriage which is no Marriage, to a silly young girl with looks, but few brains to recommend her!"

Her husband, while admitting to himself the truth of it, merely replied, "Well my dear, it is much better this way. They cannot live together, and Robert is spending all his spare time writing, so that he'll have enough material for his book. I think his troubles are likely to add depth to his work, spurring him on so that he will have something with which to impress old Master Mason Armour."

"And you have no doubt as to his success?"

"None, my dear, none whatsoever! Robert has a natural talent for making pictures with words, stories and songs, which appeal to the greatest and the least of the people. Wait you, and you will see that I am right. His gift goes beyond mere talent. It is little short of genius." His wife was unimpressed, and thought to herself that a bit less genius and a lot more *savoir-faire* regarding the fairer sex, would be better for Burns and more to her liking.

Her concern was reserved for Mary, who went about her duties cheerfully, giving no hint of her feelings, and her uncomplaining acceptance of her lot aroused in Mrs Hamilton a desire to do something to help her.

The opportunity came a few weeks later, and she sent for Mary to attend her in the Morning-Room. As they sat opposite each other, they were in complete contrast – Mrs Hamilton, plump, petite, in silk frills and flounces, hair ringleted and curled beneath her lace cap, and Mary, tall, slender in plain blue dress and spotless white apron, golden hair neatly braided round her ears.

Isabella Hamilton spoke quickly. "I expect you are wondering why I have sent for you, Mary? Well, it is to tell you that I have to visit my parents in Edinburgh to attend a celebration for my Father's birthday. Naturally, they wish the children to accompany me, especially Alexander. Now, if you wish to come with us, I shall be delighted, but there are plenty of servants in the house to look after him, and so I have another suggestion to make. How would you like to have a real holiday? Say, four weeks in Campbeltown, with your family?"

Mary stared incredulously at her mistress, a glow in her blue eyes that had long been missing, pale cheeks flushed to rose, soft lips parted in a deep breath of delight.

Observing the change in the girl, Isabella Hamilton knew that her plan was the right one, to get Mary away from all the happenings of the past months, give her time for the hurt to heal.

And so the matter was settled, and September saw Mary back in the little cottage in Ballochbrae.

CHAPTER 18

Return to Coilsfield

The first few days in Campbeltown were days of rediscovery for Mary. The house was like a doll's-house in comparison to Hamilton Hall, and what had been her room now belonged to her sister Agnes, so that they shared the same bed. But it was comforting to have Agnes's undemanding presence beside her in the night, and restful not to have to listen for Alexander's peevish cry.

Helping her Mother in the kitchen, the talk turned to Mary's brother, Rob, at present visiting relations in Greenock. Mrs Campbell told Mary, "Your Father's cousin, Peter McPherson, is a Foreman in a Shipyard, and thinks he can get an apprenticeship for Robert next year. He is to show Rob over the yard, to see if he fancies being a Carpenter."

Mary smiled, "Rab the Pirate! If he cannot sail aboard the 'Skull and Crossbones' then building ships will be the next best thing."

Her Mother laughed, "Yes, a right wild laddie was our Rab."

"But with a tender heart, Mother. I remember well one time when he had been very bad-behaved with me, would not do as he was told, and ended by yelling that he hated me. When he calmed down, he took my hand and said he was sorry, he didn't really hate me. I bent down and kissed him to his great affront, so that he growled at me, 'But don't think you can boss me, Mary Campbell, for I'm a man and you're only a lassie!'."

They laughed at the thought of it, and then Agnes Campbell looked at her daughter and asked the thing that lay heavy on her mind. "And what of your other Robert, Mary? You never speak of him, and I will say no more if it causes you any hurt."

Mary looked with unseeing eyes out of the window before turning to face her Mother. "Robert Burns is to me as part of my own self. When he is troubled, he comes . . . he used to come . . . to me for comfort, with no need of words. But now, that is over, and my heart is sore troubled, for I fear he has little peace.

At the look on Mary's face, Agnes Campbell's eyes filled with tears and she whispered, "Mary, my dear girl, never give up hope. If it is God's will, your Robert will find his way back to you."

"Yes, you are right, Mother, and we will leave everything in His hands. And see you, I am not grieving, but happy to be here with my family, and Father bringing Rab soon to make it complete."

When young Rab arrived from Greenock in his Father's company, there was rejoicing in the Campbell house that night, as they sat down to their evening meal. Preparing to say Grace, Archie Campbell looked round the table at the bowed heads of his wife and his four children, and with a full heart gave thanks to the Lord for all His blessings.

Rab kept them enthralled with his stories of Greenock, describing the busy streets where people thronged the pavements, the smell of herring in barrels of brine, the shouting of the vendors, the overall stench of ordure which lay everywhere. But then, he said, there was the other side, the tall ships in the harbour, white sails spread like wings, and the clean smell of the river. He answered his Mother's enquiring look with a smile and a nod, saying, "Aye, Mother, I so much liked the idea of being a Carpenter, that I accepted Mr McPherson's offer of an apprenticeship and will start in his Shipyard next year."

Mary wanted to know what had caused this decision, and Rab told her, "It was when I saw the keel of a boat, like the bones of a beached whale, cut and planed in the yard to become part of a whole ship, I knew that was what I wanted to do."

Laughing into Mary's eyes, he said, "When I see my first ship sail into the River of Clyde, I can imagine I'm on board, Rab-the-Pirate, bound for the China Seas!"

In the next two days, walking with Rab over well-remembered paths, paddling with him at the edge of the surfing waves, Mary experienced a feeling of contentment. Her brother, with rare understanding, said nothing of Burns, but concentrated on making her laugh at stories of his escapades in Greenock.

On the third day, her Father brought news from Ayrshire. He found Mary in the garden, gathering the last of the purple Michaelmas daisies and when he saw the brightness of her face as she called to him, he dreaded to think of her reaction to what he must tell her.

He said, quickly, "Mary, there is sad news from Mossgiel. John Burns, Robert's youngest brother, has died, with a fever of the lungs. Although he had been ailing for some time, it seems the end came suddenly."

Mary, all the colour drained from her face, whispered, "Oh no, Father, that cannot be. John is only sixteen years old, and dear to Robert's heart."

Archie Campbell led his daughter to a seat in a sun-warmed corner of the garden and told her there was no doubt of young John's death. "Robert was sent for and returned home at once. The funeral is tomorrow, and he will have to be brave, for his Mother and his family."

Bowing her head, Mary's tears overflowed as she thought of the young life, so soon ended, and the grief his death must bring to his Mother and his family.

Her Father held her in his arms, and heard her sob. "Robert will be brought low by this, Father. He always said John was a most gentle brother, the one who brought peace when quarrels arose."

Archie Campbell laid his hand on her bowed head, saying gently, "We will pray for them, Mary, that they might be comforted."

Mary sat on when her Father went indoors, thinking of Robert's grief, and with sudden insight she knew this was one time when reaching him in her thoughts was not enough. Resolutely, she went to her room and wrote down words that came from her heart.

When she had finished, she went down to the kitchen, where she found her Father and Mother talking quietly by the fire. They looked up at their daughter with loving concern, and were relieved to see that, although her eyes were still swollen with tears, they were calm and at peace.

She spoke to her Father, saying, "Father, I need your help. I have written this letter to Robert, and I ask you to post it for me when you reach Troon tomorrow."

Archie Campbell looked anxious and asked, "Mary, why must you write at all? What good can it do?"

"Father, Robert is my friend, and surely a friend stands by to help in times of trouble?" She held out her letter. "Read it, Father. I will only send it with your approval."

Archie Campbell read what was written.

Raibeart,

My thoughts are with you in your sorrow, but if there are words to take away your pain, I do not know them. All I know is, that I share it with you and say-you always in my prayers to the One who understands all, forgives all, and heals all.

From your true friend,
Mary Campbell.

Deeply moved, Archie Campbell spoke with feeling as he gave the letter into his wife's hand. "Yes, daughter, I will see that the lad gets your message, for he will have need of friends and prayers in these dark days.

Not until much later did Mary learn the effect her letter had on Robert Burns. Some days after the funeral, when he was at his lowest ebb, Mary's message came to him, at a time when his brooding melancholy held him fast. Holding the letter, recognising the writing, he was almost afraid to open it, fearing the pain of remorse her words might bring to him. A moment longer he hesitated, until his desire to reach her overcame his fear, and he opened up the page. When he saw the first word, his name in the Gaelic, he seemed to hear her speaking to him. Tears sprang to his eyes, which he dashed away with an unsteady hand so that he could read on. When he came to the end, and read "One who understands all, forgives all and heals all", Burns bowed his head against the wall and, like a dam bursting, his pent-up grief overflowed. When it was over, he was left drained and empty, yet strangely at peace. As he was to write later to Mary, her message pulled him out of the 'Slough of Despond' and back into life.

Mary received Robert's letter when she returned to

Hamilton Hall and read his last words,

> Mary,
>   I can face my future, bleak though it will
> be without you, as long as you continue to
> 'say-me' in your prayers, and keep me in a
> corner of your loving heart. You have never
> left mine,
>
>   Robert.

Tears blinded her, misting the letter, but they were tears of relief that Robert was himself again. That, and knowing he still needed her friendship, meant everything to Mary, enabling her to say that she, too, could face whatever lay ahead.

In the weeks that followed, Mary went about her work with cheerful good will, taking pleasure in nursing Alexander, happy to be back in Ayrshire, where news of Robert was not too hard to come by. She learned that he was seldom at Mossgiel, leaving the running of the farm to his brother Gilbert while he travelled the countryside in the company of Gavin Hamilton.

From Jessie Smith, she heard that Burns' 'Paper Wedding' to Jean Armour was still a closely guarded secret from Jean's Father, and that her fears about pregnancy were, so far, false alarms.

Jessie said in disgust, "It's a fushionless young woman she is, this spoiled daughter of old Armour. John Lees says she's so frightened of him she swoons at the very thought of him finding out about Robert."

Mary was puzzled at this. "But she has a paper from Robert to say they are wed. Surely she only has to show it to her Father to make everything all right."

Jessie shook her head. "It is not as simple as that,

Mary. The lass is under age, and the paper could be set aside. As well, her Father is dead set on her making a fine match with one of his great friends. Besides that, he hates everything Robert stands for, calls him ungodly, a loose-liver, mocker of the Kirk and its Elders, of which he is one! No, Mary, there is no way that Mister Armour will accept Robert Burns as Jean's husband. His pride would never allow it."

Mary bit her lip as she looked at Jessie's face, more serious than was usual with her, and she felt a pang of dismay as she thought of Robert, whose own pride was a fierce flame, likely to erupt at any attempt to slight it. Whatever was to come of this ill affair could, she felt, be nothing of good. She found herself wishing that Robert's Marriage to Jean Armour would remain a secret until his book was published. Then, perhaps, Jean's Father would accept him as her husband.

Jessie leaned across the table to enfold Mary's slender hand in her warm grasp, bringing her out of her introspective mood. Quietly she asked, "Do you and Robert never meet now, Mary? I mean. as you used to meet under the thorn tree?"

Surprised by her friend's question, Mary replied firmly. "No, Jessie, we do not. He is still my friend, but now all his loyalties must be to his wife, and it would be unseemly to hold to anyone else."

To their relief, a clatter of dishes on a tray announced Effie's arrival with tea, followed by Betty bearing a newly-baked cake, and the merry chatter which ensued smoothed over the awkwardness caused by Jessie's question.

At the end of November, Mary had an unexpected visitor at Hamilton Hall. She was taken aback to find John Lees waiting for her in the Sitting-room, his usually merry face grave and unsmiling, but not until Mrs

Hamilton left them did he reveal the reason for his visit.

Glancing at the door to make sure it was firmly closed, he answered the anxious questions behind Mary's blue eyes as he said, "Don't look so worried, lass. Robert is well, and I bring you his greetings."

As his words sank in, Mary's slender body sagged in relief, and she sank into the chair which John quickly drew forward for her. "Mary, we haven't much time, so please listen while I explain. Robert fears there is trouble brewing, trouble from Master Armour. He doesn't know yet about Jean and Robert, but his suspicions are growing that something is going on and he is hell-bent on discrediting Rob in the eyes of the Kirk. He will blackguard him with associating with loose women and having bastards on them, as well as naming him a profaner of the Church and its Ministers. That way, he could well drive Robert out of the County, and so get rid of him."

Mary drew in a quick breath and asked, "How can I help Robert, John? Is there anything I can do?"

Disliking what he had to say next, John Lees slid his eyes away from her face, "Robert is afraid that old Armour intends to name you in his calumnations, Mary. It is no secret that Gavin Hamilton employed you at Rob's behest, and you can see where that might lead."

Mary's blue eyes flashed fire and she spoke heatedly. "Surely this Mr Armour would not dare to speak out against a man of Mr Hamilton's standing!"

John shook his head. "Master Mason Armour has no regard for Gavin, high position or no. He considers him as ungodly as Robert, and has caused him to be brought to the Sinner's Stool for profaning the Sabbath. He would be more than happy to smear him further by accusing him of aiding and abetting Robert in his association with you."

Horrified, Mary exclaimed, "But never has there been anything between us but friendship only. Oh, this man must be truly wicked, to spread such evil lies."

"Truly spoken, lass! Now, here is Robert's plan to take you out of Armour's reach. Your old position at Coilsfield will become vacant at the end of next month, and the Montgomeries will be delighted to have you back."

Mary hesitated, saying slowly, "I would not wish to appear ungrateful to Mistress Hamilton, nor to leave her without a Nurse for Alexander."

"Mary, Mr Hamilton has it all arranged, for he agrees with Robert that you must not be exposed to Armour's malice. He will explain everything to his wife, and a new Nursemaid will be engaged before you leave. That is, if you agree to go. I can tell you, Jessie is over the moon at the thought of getting you back! And, lass, Rob said to tell you that your departure to Coilsfield will bring him great peace of mind. He also bade me repeat to you these words, and, closing his eyes, he recited: "Though worlds divide us, nothing can separate mind from mind, nor heart from heart, when these are joined in purest love."

When Mary heard this, and when John Lees asked if she had an answer for Robert, she replied, "Tell him he shall have his peace of mind and . . . that I understand his message, and thank him for it."

And so it was arranged. And at the end of December, Mary said goodbye to her companions at Hamilton Hall, whose genuine regrets at losing her were offset by the warmth of her reception at Montgomerie House, where her old friends waited to greet her and bid her "Welcome back".

CHAPTER 19
The Storm Breaks

The keen, glittering frost of January, which had lasted since the New Year, gave way to days of unrelieved greyness. At Montgomerie House, lamps were lit early and burned all day, to offset the darkness outside, and great fires of logs and coal sent out welcome heat against the bone-chilling damp which hung everywhere.

Mary was glad of Betty's cheerful prattle as they worked together in the dairy, churning out butter, putting up cheeses, skimming off rich cream, some of which Jessie would serve to put on their porridge, "to keep your strength up" as she said. Now, as the short day drew to a close, Betty exclaimed in exasperation, "Och, it's no use, Mary! We cannot see what we're doing, with all these shadows jinking in between the lamps. Let's finish up here and get back to the kitchen." As they placed the dishes of cream on the slate-shelves, Betty suddenly asked, "What do you wish for most in this new year of 1786, Mary?"

Taken by surprise, Mary answered without thinking, "I wish for happiness for all my friends and whatever they most desire."

Betty knew she was thinking of Robert Burns, but was wise enough not to mention his name. Instead, she laughed and leaned close to whisper, "Well, here is one friend who thanks you, for I do believe I'm going to get my heart's desire. Can you guess what that might be?"

Mary gazed into Betty's laughing eyes, and knew at once. "Betty, you mean that you and Davie are betrothed? But I thought this could not be, not for many years, you said?"

Betty whirled round in a skipping, dancing step, and came to throw her arms about Mary's neck. "Och, it's all a big secret yet, but I've just got to tell you! Davie's uncle is Head-Coachman down in the Borders, and he's to retire at the end of the year. Well, he's in need of an assistant and has spoken for Davie and, when he retires, Davie has the chance of his job. There's a house to go with it and more money, so we'd be able to marry this time next year."

Mary was truly pleased at Betty's news and promised to be Maid-of-Honour at her Wedding. She smiled when she was sworn to silence, thinking it would be difficult for Betty to keep her secret for very long. As she dwelled on this good omen for her wish, she hoped it would extend to Robert, bringing him happiness with his Jean, an acceptance of their Marriage by her Father and a settling-down to married life. More, she wished for his success with his book, knowing how much the recognition of his work meant to him.

The next weeks were busy ones at Montgomerie House, with a succession of glittering Balls, Receptions and Suppers, which occupied the entire staff from morning to night, so that Mary was thankful to fall into bed where she slept without dreams.

The dark, grey wetness of late January gave way to a cold, sunny February, with blue skies and white snowdrops appearing under the hedges. Mary delighted in the change and walked the hills with Jessie whenever their duties allowed, breathing in air so cold and pure it seared the lungs as it reached them. On one such walk, Mary raised her face to the sky and laughed aloud to feel the wind tugging at her bonnet. Swiftly, she loosened the ribbons and shook her hair free of its braids, causing it to be blown every which way to Jessie's scandalisation. But Mary paid no heed to her scolding, grasping her by the hand, pulling her into a run down the grassy slope till they finished up against a thick hedge, panting and exhilarated.

Mary, not hampered by excess weight as Jessie was, recovered first and as she pinned up her hair she said breathlessly, "Now admit you, Jessie, you feel like a little girl again."

Holding her side and giving a gasp as she got her second wind, Jessie suddenly laughed, "Och, it's clean daft you are, Mary Campbell, kicking up your heels like a Spring lamb and me running like a gyte sheep beside ye! It is thankful I am there's nobody to see us, or we'd be shut in the Asylum, that we would." Arm-in-Arm they resumed their walk, headed for home now and much refreshed by their run. Jessie cast a sidelong glance at Mary's glowing face, and wondered whether or not to tell her the latest news of Robert, then decided against it.

No use breaking into Mary's happy mood until she had to. After all, as John Lees said, Jean Armour had had more than one false alarm, and this could well be another, brought on by the sheer terror of her Father finding out. With hardly a pause, it seemed, February melted into March, with windless, sunny days filled with golden daffodils and green fields filled with frolicking lambs. But the peaceful days were destined not to last, breaking into howling gales and slashing rain, tearing off flower petals and buds before they had fully opened.

At the same time, a storm of another kind swept furiously over Jean Armour and Robert Burns, repercussions of which resounded throughout the countryside. Almost at once, news of this event was brought to Montgomerie House by Effie. Her sister, Kirsty, worked in the Armour household and, on a visit home, Effie had found her cowering by the fire, white-faced and deaf to a barrage of questions from her family. Shouting at them to keep quiet, Effie thrust a mug of hot tea into Kirsty's hand and stood over her while she drank it. Gradually, the girl recovered from her fright and was able to answer her Mother's anxious question as to whether or not she had been sacked. "No, but I've to stay here till I'm sent for. No' juist me, every wan o' us except the Cook."

Seeing that the volume of enquiries was likely to addle Kirsty's wits, Effie took over. She hushed everyone up, and spoke coaxingly. "Just begin at the beginning, Kirsty, and tell us what you can. Take your time, lassie, and nobody will interrupt you." This last accompanied by a warning glare at the avid, open-mouthed faces of the others.

Kirsty's story was told in simple, rustic words, but so startling was the gist of it that it held the listeners spellbound. The account of illicit love, sin, illegitimate bairns, was nothing new to the common folk, but that it concerned the grand house of the important Mr Armour, wealthy man of business, Master Mason of the town Lodge, Elder of the Kirk, his lady wife and his idolised daughter, Miss Jean! These facts electrified them all and had them hanging on Kirsty's every word.

"Ye ken Miss Jean's a bonny wee thing, wi' plenty o' lads oglin' her, but whispers have been heard aboot wan in particular, the fairmer o' Mossgiel, Robert Burns. Weel, something was said to her Faither this morn' an' he came stamping hame wi' a face like a thunder-cloud demandin' that his wife and daughter be brought to the parlour right that meenit. Weel, the maid was sae frightened by his black looks she forgot to shut the door and we could see him stottin' aboot mutterin' and chuggin' at his long beard as if he'd tear it oot by the roots. We were spyin' oot o' a crack in the kitchen door when doon the stairs cam' Miss Jean and her mither, hingin' on tae each ither and near fainting, faces white as tallow, eyes bulgin' oot o' their sockets wi' fright.

"The meenit he saw Miss Jean, he gripped her by the arms, looked her up and looked her down, and then Mrs Armour shut the door an' we couldnae see ony mair. But we heard him, the hale street must hae heard him, roarin' at her like a mad bull to gie the lie to what had been said, that she was havin' a bairn to that blackguard, Robert Burns. Miss Jean and her mither were greetin' and pleadin' wi' him tae listen to them and we heard Miss Jean tell him, Aye, she was wi' child, but was a marrit wumman and had a paper to prove it. That was when it happened . . . the roarin' stopped, we heard a queer gurglin' sound as if he was chokin' and a terrible crash. Mrs Armour cam' fleein' oot cryin' for John the Coach to bring the Doctor and there wis the Maister lyin' on the carpet under the table he'd pulled over and Miss Jean standin' like a stookie gazin' doon at him. The Doctor and John came and got him onto the couch, and the Doctor tellt Mrs Armour it wasnae serious, juist a fit brocht on by temper and to keep him quiet an' nae arguin' aboot onything."

Here Kirsty stopped to get her breath back and said, "An' that's a'!" Which bald statement roused a fury of indignation in her audience, with Effie telling her, "That cannae be all, ye daft lassie! What happened when your

Master recovered, and why were you all sent away? And what more did you hear about Robert Burns?"

Kirsty, happily drinking another mug of tea, had little interest in the after-events as told to them by the Parlour-maid but she repeated what she had heard.

"Och, when he cam' oot o' his fit, he took the paper frae Miss Jean and cut oot the names on it, and made her swear on the Bible it was false. She's tae be sent away tae an' auld auntie in Paisley, an' she's tae confess tae the Kirk aboot her an' Robert Burns an' sit on the Cutty Stool. Och, she grat awfie sore but she did as she was telt. An' we were a' sent hame because the hoose is tae be shut up while the Armours are in Paisley."

This was the story which Effie carried back to Montgomerie House and to Mary it seemed that her worst fears for Robert were realised. She had no doubt that someone would have brought him the news of Armour's repudiation of him and her heart ached for his hurt. She also felt a deep pity for the young Jean Armour, a mere girl, having to face the violent rage of her Father with none to protect her.

Some days later, Mary had a visit from John Lees. She was in the Dairy, working on her own with no sign of Betty, to John's evident relief as he looked around him. Anxious for news of Robert, she was almost afraid to ask as she waited for Lees to speak. Coming close to her, he said quietly, "Mary, Robert asks you to wait until he can come to you and explain matters. You will have heard what has happened?"

Mary nodded, her eyes urging him to go on. "Aye, well, it's bad for Rob, there's no denying. He's heard through Masonic whispers that old Armour has vowed vengeance on him. Now that he's got Jean safely out of the way in Paisley, the wicked old de'il has sworn to have

Robert locked up in jail and he's to sue him for all the siller he's to get for his book, to pay for Jean's Lying-in."

The colour drained from Mary's face at John's words. "But how can that be? Robert gave Jean a Marriage-paper and even though her Father denies it, Robert will still honour it."

"Lassie, you have not understood. The auld man and his daughter have foresworn the 'Marriage' and will never acknowledge Rob as husband or son-in-law. To auld Armour, it's an unholy relationship, the seduction of his innocent, under-age daughter, with an ungodly lecher. No, Mary, the only thing for Robert is to get clean away until he can sort things out. But he'll tell you all about it when he can arrange to meet you, and that will be soon."

With that, he slipped out of the door and was gone, leaving Mary with many unanswered questions. But, to offset these, was the glad knowledge that soon she would see Robert for herself, and hear from his own lips how he fared. Montgomerie House was filled with rumours and counter-rumours: the Armours were back in Ayr (this confirmed by Effie's sister Kirsty); Robert Burns was in jail; Burns had disappeared; Jean Armour was missing from her Aunt's home in Paisley, kidnapped by her lover; old Armour had threatened to shoot Burns. As the tales grew and got wilder, Mary refused to listen to them, but waited and worried in silence. One consolation was a letter from her Father, stating his support for Robert and his condemnation of Armour's rejecting of the Marriage-paper and his subsequent pursuit of Burns "out of wicked spite and greed for money".

Her brother, Rab, had added a sentence which brought a smile to Mary's lips. "If I could tell you all I feel for this Master Armour, it would set Father's letter in such a blaze only a black cinder would reach you."

One fine afternoon John Lees arrived at the House, ostensibly to visit Jessie. He kept up a merry chatter as he drank his ale and ate the scones, new-baked from the oven, but to all the eager questions about Burns, he had little to tell, to the vociferous disappointment of the company. Mary said nothing, but her spirits sank to a low ebb at the lack of news. When John remarked on the fine Spring weather and asked Jessie to go for a walk, he included Mary in his invitation. But she declined to accompany them, until Jessie added her coaxings by saying the fresh air would put some colour in her cheeks. Listlessly, Mary went with them. She did not notice that their way suddenly diverged from the main path into a left-hand fork where, just over the hill, the square tower of a ruined castle could be seen. She first became aware of it when John's hand on her arm halted her steps. A faint curiosity lit her blue eyes as she saw the old Keep, and wondering, she turned to look at Lees. John, eyes dancing, a broad grin on his face, was nodding his head like a Chinese Mandarin, and Mary gave a sudden gasp of understanding.

Jessie never forgot the transformation that came over Mary as she whispered one work, "Robert." Joy shone from her eyes, colour flooded her cheeks, and her dazzling smile rivalled the sunlight.

John laughed with her as he told her, "Aye, lass, it's Rob! He's waiting for you in the Old Chapel, and nobody must know he's here. That's why I couldn't tell you before, and when I look at you now, I know I was right. You would have given the show away, without a doubt! We will walk with you as far as the Castle, and wait to see you safely back to the House." On winged feet, Mary flew ahead, never pausing till she reached the ruined

Chapel. There, she stopped for one brief moment, then, unhesitatingly, she walked through the arched portals, passing from bright sunlight to the dimness of shadows. When her eyes adjusted to the gloom, she made out a tall figure, outlined against an open embrasure, and knew it was Robert.

He saw her at the same moment, heard the quick intake of her breath before she spoke his name, and hands outstretched, each to the other, they came together. Mary's slender fingers crushed in his powerful grasp, for a long poignant, moment, blue eyes gazed deep into brown, until at last Burns breathed her name and bent his head to press a passionate kiss on each soft palm.

Seated on a stone bench on the wall, Mary listened to his quick-pouring words, at first hearing little of their meaning as she drank in the vibrant tones of his voice, and traced the lines of each well-remembered feature. Just to have him close to her, after so long a separation, was enough and more than enough. Then, moved by the urgency of his speech, her attention was caught and held.

"Never will I forgive that man for what he has done to me and his daughter. He has denied our Marriage-Bond, even though he knows Jean is to have my child, and has sent her away to 'hide her shame' as he puts it." Mary could hear his bitterness, the wounded pride and fierce resentment at Armour's repudiation of him.

He went on, "He has sworn to sue me for Jean's keep, and the child's when it comes. He's heard I'll likely get a goodly sum when my book is published, and he means to have it all, or clap me in jail, until I pay up. Well, that I will never do! Had he accepted our Marriage, I would have given Jean a home and everything her heart desired, but as it is, he'll not see one guinea of my money, and if he thinks to clap me in jail, he'll have to catch me first." Disturbed by a new hardness in his voice, Mary turned to face him, and bit her lip as she noted the glitter of his eyes and the aggressive thrust to his jaw.

Then, in a moment, drawn by her worried gaze, the hardness was swept away and he looked at her with such love that she had to lower her eyes as a warm blush crimsoned her cheeks. Smiling down at her averted face, he touched his lips to her soft, golden hair and, stroking it gently, told her, "One good thing has come out of this sorry business, Mary, and that is that soon I will be free. Will you wait for me, my dearest lass, until I no longer need to hide from old Armour and his Watchers?"

At this, Mary raised her head to look at him and, with no hesitation, gave her answer, "Yes, Robert, I will wait and count it no hardship till you come to me."

A low whistle from outside the Chapel warned Burns it was time to leave. Drawing Mary to her feet, he clasped her in his arms as if he'd never let her go, saying, "Och, lass, I have no time to tell you all that is in my heart, but I will send word by John when I am safely away. You know that I will come to you whenever I can, and never forget to 'say-me' in your prayers."

With this, he stooped to press his lips to hers and they clung together for one timeless moment. Another, louder whistle came from outside, alerting Burns to his danger, but unable and unwilling to tear himself from Mary's arms, he refused to heed it. It was she who proved the stronger of the two as she gently released herself from his embrace. She stepped back and softly told him, "'Tis time to leave, Robert, so go you with God and Him with you to keep you safe wherever you may be."

Without flinching, she watched him stumble away from the dim Chapel into the sunlight, and only when she was sure he had gone did she venture out. Jessie Smith saw at once that this was a changed Mary. Although her expression was serious, there was a new, soft light in her blue eyes, and a new maturity in her bearing. On the walk back to Montgomerie House, Lees told Mary that Robert's letters would be addressed to him and then brought to her to avert any suspicion from the Watchers. Before going to bed that night, Mary gazed out at the moonlit sky and, seeing one pale star, wondered if Robert also looked at it shining there. She wondered, too, when and where they would next meet, and whispering an extra prayer for his safety, with one last look at the star, she bade him a silent "goodnight".

CHAPTER 20

The Time of
the Singing Birds

It taxed all of Mary's fortitude to carry on her daily work with an unruffled calm, when it seemed that the varied April weather exactly matched her moods. One moment there was warm sun, blue skies and scudding white clouds; the next, darkness, driving hail and bitter East winds – like her hopes and fears, moving from elation to uncertainty and despair when no word arrived from Robert.

She waited in vain for a visit from John Lees, as he too, seemed to have vanished. Jessie, as much in the dark as Mary, sent Effie on a visit to her sister Kirsty, with instructions to find out what was happening in the Armour household. Waiting for Effie's return, Mary found herself in a state of fidgets. She picked things up only to put them down again, didn't hear Jessie when she spoke, and jumped every time the door opened. Only when Jessie firmly pushed her into a chair at the table and handed her a steaming cup, did she relax. She sipped the hot tea and looked at Jessie with an apologetic smile, saying, "What is wrong with me tonight, I am not knowing."

Jessie leaned over to pat her hand, "I think I can guess, Mary. It's the not-knowing that keeps your heart unsteady, one minute up, the next down!"

At that moment the door slammed open and Effie stumbled in, clutching her bonnet against the tug of the wind, gasping, "Och, what a night! I thought I'd be blown richt off my feet into the sky like the Witches at Hallowe'en!"

Jessie snorted, "Away wi' ye and don't be sae daft! Come, sit you down and drink this and tell us a' your news." Mary pulled out a chair as Effie removed her bonnet and shawl and Jessie poured from the big brown teapot. Effie drank her tea with loud gulps and when she finished, she gave a long sigh of repletion and pushed her cup over to be refilled. This time she was content to sip and to talk!

"Well, here's what Kirsty told me, and it's no very much. She says the auld man has buttoned up his mouth and shut his ears to a' the gossip. Mind you, it would be a brave man or a daftie that wid daur speir him aboot his dochter and Robert Burns, so glowerin fierce are his eyes an' his big beard a' fuzzed up wi' rage."

Here she paused to reach out for a scone and Mary asked anxiously, "Did he not say anything about Robert?"

"Aye, he did, but nothing good. Kirsty said half-a-dozen of his grand friends called yesterday afternoon and she had to carry in drinks. Some o' them were ower free wi' the whisky and began to speir Master Armour about Robert's book. They wanted to know if it was soon to be printed and if it would make much money. The old man telt them the more it made the better he'd be pleased, as he meant to have the lot for what had been done to his daughter.

"One o' the men laughed, and said first he'd have to catch him and anither asked was it true that Burns had jouked the Watchers and had got to Kilmarnock.

That near choked the Master and he showed them all the door, quiet-like, and then cursed them a' wi' terrible oaths, and him a Kirk Elder!"

Mary drew in a deep breath, feeling a load had been lifted from her. Robert was well, and free to move about in spite of the Watchers, and she knew that he would get word to her somehow. She prayed it would be soon.

Two days later coming out of Church with Jessie, she saw the familiar figure of John Lees walking towards them, and heard his voice raised in greeting, "Good morning, ladies, it is sorry I am not to have been with you in the Kirk, but with your permission I will give myself the pleasure of escorting you home." Something about his smiling face caused Mary's heart to beat faster, and she knew that he had news for her. John tucked her hand under his arm, and pressed it gently while seemingly intent on Jessie at his other side, and then she was certain. She understood that he would give nothing away while the others were close enough to overhear him, and forced herself to act normally as they strolled along the sunlit path.

When they reached Montgomerie House, Jessie sent Mary to fetch a jug of milk and a dish of cream from the Dairy, while she set out the food. John immediately said he'd go with her, which offer Mary gladly accepted. In the coolness of the Buttery, Mary lifted down from the shelf a large enamelled jug of new milk, and a deep bowl of yellow cream over which she spread a clean muslin cloth. John moved quickly to stand beside her, and without a word, handed over a folded piece of paper.

Mary slipped it into her pocket, asking only one question, "Is he well?"

"Yes, he is well, and quite safe. Now quickly, before we arouse any suspicions, let us get back to the kitchen."

The Love of Highland Mary

Lifting the heavy jug, he led the way out of the Dairy, speaking loudly of nothing in particular, as Mary followed him, answering she knew not what in reply. Somehow, she ate the food which Jessie set before her, joining in the talk around the table, until at last she was able to escape to her room. Sitting on the edge of the bed, she waited till her hands stopped shaking before she carefully broke the thin wax seal on the back of the paper. Gently, she opened out the four points and found enclosed something which puzzled her. With the tip of her finger, she touched it, and as it fluttered lightly onto her outstretched palm, recognition dawned on her.

It was the heart-shaped petal of a white rose. Looking closer, she could see that the satiny surface was marred by black marks, and as she studied them understanding dawned on her. The marks formed four words, in Robert's writing, one under the other, spelling out his message, "You have my heart." Four words which told her everything she wanted to know, words which she whispered back to him.

She was pulled out of her dreams by Jessie's voice, calling, "Mary, John would say goodbye to you before he leaves. Come away now, and do not keep him waiting." Mary closed the rose-petal into its paper and placed in in her box, laying it lovingly beside her Bibles. John and Jessie looked up as she came into the kitchen and both were struck by the change in her. To Jessie she seemed to be lit from within, but to John, the glow in her eyes, the blush on her cheeks, spoke of a woman in love. They were filled with curiosity as to what Robert had written in his letter, but Mary kept her silence in a way which made it impossible to question her.

That Tuesday evening, unusually warm for late April, Jessie decided to pour out glasses of cool, homemade Dandelion wine, instead of tea. Mary was in the act of handing round the drinks when Willie the Gardener's words caused her arm to jerk violently, spilling the wine onto the table.

"Aye," he said, "ye'll never guess whit I heard this morning about Master Armour and Robert Burns."

With this, he paused to drink thirstily, to the frustration of his listeners, especially Mary, who was hard put to keep a calm face as she waited for him to go on. At last Willie, never one to be hurried, even when nudged by Jean, resumed his tale. "Where was I, now? Och aye, I was telling you about old Armour and oor Rabbie. Well, it seems the old man has called off his Watchdogs, so whit dae ye think o' that?"

There was a stunned silence, followed by a babble of voices – "He's too mean to go on paying" . . . "It's a trick to lure Burns into a trap" . . . and, from Jean, "Likely he's relented and means to acknowledge the Marriage, now he's sniffed out the possibility of siller from Rob's book."

Only Jessie voiced the commonsense view, saying impatiently, "Och, it is daft you all are, that you cannot see what's behind it! Aye, Jean, it's the money he's after, right enough, and he cannot have that if there's no book. And if Robert cannot get his poems to the Printer, there never will be a book. That is as plain as the nose on your face! As for accepting Rob as his son-in-law, that stiff-necked auld De'il would sooner hang himself!" There were murmers of agreement all round as the others accepted the truth of Jessie's words. In the days that followed, Mary spent all her time in the Dairy, glad of work that kept her hands busy and her mind occupied, tiring her so that she went to bed and slept without dreams.

Jessie found herself wishing that John Lees would pay them a visit, to tell them what Robert's plans were now that he didn't have to hide from the Watchers. It seemed that Jessie's wish was father to the thought, for the very next day she heard footsteps and a familiar, merry whistling as Lees approached the open kitchen door. To his pleased astonishment, he found himself almost lifted off his feet as Jessie burst on him like a very tornado, grabbing his arms and demanding to know what had kept him.

Laughing, he circled Jessie's ample waist with both arms, saying, "Well, well! This is what I call a welcome and demands a proper greeting!" With this, he bent to kiss her lips but got only her cheek as she twisted her face away, scolding him half in affection, half in reproof.

"Och, stop your nonsense in front of all the others." John looked to see if she was joking. "What others? I see only Effie. Where is Mary? And Betty and Jean?"

"They are not finished their work yet, as you ought to know, so sit yourself down and give us your chaff. Where is Robert these days? Will he come back now old Armour has called off his Watchers? And is there really going to be a book?"

Pretending to gasp for breath, John leaned back in his chair and protested, "Jessie lass, one question at a time, if you please!" Then, with a quick glance at Effie's interested face, he said, "I do not know where Rob is at this moment, but I don't doubt he'll be back, if only to make sure there will be a book.

"The Printer in Kilmarnock, John Wilson, reports that orders are pouring in, but he can do nothing until Robert brings him more of the poems and songs he has been writing."

Mary, accompanied by Betty and Jean, heard John's

last words as they entered the kitchen and she could not control the hot blush that crimsoned her cheeks. Luckily, the others were too intent on John to notice, and in the general hustle to set out the meal, she had time to recover her composure. As they ate cold meat and floury potatoes served with Jessie's special mustard sauce, Mary was glad of the many questions asked by the others about Robert and Jean Armour. She learned that Jean was still with her Aunt in Paisley, that she was well enough but never allowed out by herself, that her name was never mentioned in her Father's house and that, certainly, Robert had not once attempted to see her. While the others blamed her and said it was all her own fault, Mary felt sorry for the young girl. If her Father really cared for her as a Father should, he would have put her happiness before anything else. Jessie looked at Mary's withdrawn expression, and guessed that it had to do with mention of Jean Armour. Who, she asked herself, but kind-hearted Mary, would give a second thought to a silly lassie who hadn't enough backbone to defy her Father and stick to her man? Rising from the table, she brought the conversation to an end and John Lees made his goodbyes.

At the door, he bent to kiss Mary's cheek and, unseen by the others, pressed a folded paper into her hand. Mary's fingers closed convulsively over it and she closed her eyes for a brief second, glad that the ones at her back could not see her face. The fresh evening breeze brought the scent of lilacs and wallflowers, and she breathed deeply of the mingled, heady perfumes, until her mind cleared and her composure returned. Murmuring to Jessie that she would pick mint and parsley for tomorrow's garnish, she escaped into the herb garden, and soon had gathered a handful of each. When she was certain there was no-one else about, she at last allowed herself to open her letter.

The message was brief, with no salutation and no signature, but it was enough to fill her with joy.

Tomorrow evening at 7, the Thorn Tree.

Pressing her lips to the beloved writing, Mary placed the note out of sight, against her heart. So full of high emotion was she, that she lingered in the garden, restlessly crushing a sprig of mint between her fingers and inhaling its sharp, pungent smell. Gradually, she gained control of her feelings and went in to join the others, to all appearances her usual calm, unruffled self.

Next morning, she was up before the birds began their morning-chorus, and flew about her tasks until Betty exclaimed, "For goodness sake, Mary. What's got into you? If you don't slow down, you'll sour the cream, the rate your going at it, and Jessie won't thank you if that happens! It's hard enough keeping it fresh in this hot spell. It's more like the end of July than the end of April."

Mary started guiltily, and hastily apologised, "It is sorry I am, Betty, to be upsetting you. It is the heat that is bothering me, the way it makes the cattle kick up their heels and race to find a shady spot." Good-natured Betty accepted the apology, and poured two glasses of frothing buttermilk. Refreshed by the cool drink, they carried on with their jobs and now Mary sensibly kept pace with Betty, to their mutual satisfaction. At half-past-six, when the evening meal was over, Mary was dismayed to find that Jessie proposed to accompany her on her walk, but could think of no excuse to put her off. They made an attractive pair as they set off, plump, black-haired Jessie in pink; slender, golden-haired Mary in blue.

Linking arms, Jessie chattered blithely about nothing

in particular, seeming not to notice Mary's silence. When they were out of sight of the house, with a complete change of voice, she said, "Mary, it is all right. I know about your meeting with Robert. John told me. We will make sure no-one comes near while you are together, and I am sorry there was no chance to tell you sooner."

Mary felt a surge of relief and grasped Jessie's hand as she confessed, "It is glad I am that you know, Jessie. I was afraid to say a word in case I brought troubles to Robert."

Jessie reassured her that no such thing would happen and pointed down the path, "Look, here comes John now, whistling like a linty."

Mary asked anxiously, "But where is Robert? Why isn't he with John?" Drawing Jessie with her, she hastened her steps and before a word of greeting was exchanged, burst out, "Has something happened to Robert?"

Swiftly Lees assured her this was not so, adding, with a glance over his shoulder to indicate the thorn tree, "You will find him where he said he would be."

On hearing this, Mary would have rushed ahead, had John not prevented her, saying quietly, "Steady, lass, we'll walk on together, the three of us. Just be easy, now."

As they came to the thorn tree, the branches parted and Robert stood before them. With eyes only for each other, neither Mary nor Burns saw the others step aside. For a long, silent moment they looked, then taking her hand in his, he held back the sweet-smelling screen of flowers for her to enter. As one in a dream, Mary gazed at his face as if she could not believe he was really there.

Burns held her hands and kissed them, murmuring inarticulate words of endearment until he suddenly straightened up, drew in a deep breath and with an obvious effort, spoke softly. "Mary, my dearest lass, I have so much to tell you, and so little time. I don't know how long I'll be free of Armour's Watchers, although I believe he will hold them off until my book is ready. But now I hear he's stirred up the Kirk and the Ministers against me and that can only bring more trouble."

"But how so, Robert? What is it you have done to upset the Church?"

"There is a charge of sinning with his daughter, and there are the poems I've written, poking fun at the Holy Willie's and the two-faced Elders, who denounce sinners in public and are the biggest rogues of all in private! But what counts now is that I have to keep a safe distance from them all, until I have enough poems and songs for John Wilson to make into a book. And then I will make certain that sour old Devil, Armour, will never get his hands on one penny of my money."

Seeing his face darken, Mary gently touched his hand until he smiled at her and said, "Now, enough of that, lass. Let us talk of you and me. I have to tell you, Mary, my feelings for you go far beyond friendship, and now, at last, I can say what has always been in my heart. I love you, my dearest lass, and would know if you love me, not as a friend, but as a woman loves a man. If that is so, will you be my wife, when I can come to you freely?"

At first, hearing his words, Mary trembled, afraid of the welter of emotions that stirred in her breast, but now, as she looked at his loving, pleading face, her fears vanished and, placing her hands in his, she gave him her answer. "I do love you, Robert, in the way you desire, and to be your wife I would wait for you and count it no hardship." When he heard this, Burns gave a long sigh of relief and his joy at her words found expression in the kisses he rained upon her face, touching her brow, her closed eyes, and gently, her soft lips. Mary's response was both yielding and timid, and sensing this, he drew back and began to speak.

"Now that we are promised, dear heart of my heart, we will have a Betrothal, but of this I will write to you later. Also, I will send a letter to your Father, asking his permission and his Blessing on our Marriage."

There was no more time left to them as they heard the voices of Jessie and John, and no need to proclaim their news. Their radiant faces, Burns' proprietorial air, Mary's blushing cheeks and downcast eyes, said it all. As April gave way to May, now began for Mary the 'time of the singing birds' when life was a dream, and the dream was Love.

CHAPTER 21

The Gypsy's Fortune

In Montgomerie House, Mary's glowing looks gave rise to much speculation, with Betty and Effie bombarding her with questions. Had she heard from Robert, and if not, why not? When was he coming back? Why was he still hiding when there were no Watchers? Getting no response from Mary, they soon tired of pestering her and found diversion in talking of their own affairs.

Betty was overflowing with news as she related that Davie was soon to set off to his job in the Borders. "I'm to join him in January, and we'll be married here first, and you've all to come to the Wedding."

This brought an envious response from Effie. "Och, you're lucky, Betty, so you are. I wish I had a lad, but Jimmie will hae naething tae dae wi' me. He says ah'm no' bonnie, but sure ah'm bonnier that ah used tae be, am ah no' Mary?"

Kind-hearted Mary was quick to reassure her. "Yes indeed, Effie, you are quite changed for the better."

"Aye," put in Jessie, "you've filled out, not sic a ruchle o' bones, more cushiony like."

Effie cheered up at this, but sighed, "Weel then, hoo can ah make Jimmie like me?"

Betty, hands on hips, advised, "For a start, stop chasin' after him. Who is he to talk? Sic a queer looking craiter wi' his squint an' his big ears, he should be thankful anybody fancies him! You'll find a better lad than Jimmie, just you wait and see."

As Betty finished speaking, there came a knock at the open door and a foreign-sounding voice was heard to say, "Who will buy my pretty ribbons, to make a true Lover's knot, or golden combs from Spain to crown you like a queen?" Startled, they turned to stare at the Gypsy who stood, half-in. half-out, of the doorway, a basket of trinkets on her arm. Tall, thin, olive-skinned, with snapping black eyes, she was an exotic figure, festooned in strings of multi-coloured beads which fell to her waist, below which was a crimson skirt of many flounces. Large gold circles in her ears completed her costume, and for a moment, staring at her, they were frozen there like a scene from a Tableau.

Then, the spell was broken. The Gypsy woman smiled, and looking from one to the other, said, "Tell your fortunes, my ladies, if you cross my palm with silver." With one accord, the three girls turned to look at Jessie, whose 'yea or nay' could send this foreign creature packing in an instant. They saw their own feelings reflected in her face, half-scared, half-fascinated, and then, recovering, she spoke.

"There's no silver here to cross your palm, my woman, so it is wasting your time you are with your begging."

With a hiss like a striking snake, the Gypsy spat at her, "I am not a beggar, nor am I a Tinker body. I am a Romany and trade honestly. If you have no silver, any small coin will do. If you wish to look at my goods, I sell for a fair price. The choice is yours."

Her anger had disappeared and her proud speech impressed the women more than they cared to admit.

Suddenly, Jessie made up her mind. "Very well, then, we will look at your trinkets, so come away in." With a cat-like grace the Gypsy swung her heavy basket onto her hip and, placing it on the table, stepped aside to let them examine the contents. Effie picked out a knot of bright red ribbons and wondered aloud if she could afford them. Betty, with her Wedding in mind, chose broad white silk and a strip of white lace, while Jessie, without hesitation, reached for a velvet cluster in deep rose pink. Mary, like Jessie, knew what she wanted, deep blue ribbons, the blue that Robert always said matched her eyes. Then, tempted, she decided to buy a skein of fine white thread to crochet a wide collar and cuffs for the dress she intended to make, a dress the exact shade of the ribbons.

While they paid for their ribbons, Jessie poured cool drinks from a jug of Elderflower wine, which the Gypsy drank thirstily. Setting down her glass, she asked who would be the first to have her fortune read. Glancing sideways at each other, no one volunteered until, giggling nervously, Effie thrust out her hand, palm upward to show the coin held there. With a swift movement, the Romany leaned to move the seat back and rejected the outstretched hand, saying, "No, both hands I must see."

Obediently, Effie held them out to her, and was told, "Left hand shows lines you are born with; right hand alters with life." Taking the coin, she traced a design across the right palm, muttering some foreign words as she did so. Then, releasing the left hand, she peered closely at the lines on the right, "Two men I see, one close and not for you. One, still to come, will be your fate. Many children you will have, and happiness to please you more than riches."

Effie open-mouthed in wonder, made way for Betty. The Gypsy went through the same procedure, tracing a line and nodding to herself. "There is someone near to you, whose name begins with the letter D, and I see a ring which signifies a union. There is a journey before you and a new life opening. Three children you will rear, and live long with your man."

Next came Jessie, whose sceptical look was not lost on the Romany. She gazed at the well-fleshed pink palm, saying nothing for a moment, then, "I see the initial J; it is someone who wishes to come close to you, but for him you have only friendship. You have boxed lines, here, which show you wish to guard your dreams." At this, Jessie's hand jerked as if she would pull it away, but the thin, strong fingers held tight as the voice proceeded. "A dark stranger will come into your life from over the sea to make your dream come true. Look for the initial L. I see no children, but also, no regrets. You will share love enough."

Jessie rose to her feet with alacrity, relieved that her secret wish to have a place of her own and a husband, had not been revealed. That it was known to the Romany she did not doubt, as she met her all-knowing look, and the quick dip of her head.

Now it was Mary's turn, but when she made no move, the Gypsy looked at her with sudden keen interest. Expecting to see a timid, fearful creature, instead she encountered Mary's calm, steadfast gaze, that neither accepted nor rejected her. Quietly speaking as to an equal, the Gypsy said, "You are not from these parts. You are as alien as I am, with a speech as foreign to the tongue. Answer me in your own language if I speak the truth."

Softly, in the Gaelic, Mary replied, "You speak the truth."

"Your speech is that which I have heard in the far North, from a people as ancient and as proud as my own. Come, I will read your fortune without payment, for the bond that is between us." Spreading Mary's slim. narrow hands, she swept them both with one swift glance, after which, all expression left her face. Without looking at Mary, her voice empty of any trace of feeling, she asked, "What age are you, child?"

Quietly, Mary answered, "Twenty three years I will have soon." Then the Gypsy did a strange thing, she very gently laid Mary's left hand, palm down, on the table and concentrated her whole attention on the right hand.

With a feeling of unease, Jessie remembered her words, "The left hand shows the life we are born with, the right is what we make of it."

Head bowed, voice expressionless, the Romany spoke, "I see a letter, soon to arrive, beside the initial R. Vows exchanged over running water. Three books are given, books important to the vows. You will cross the sea, and save the life of someone who is kin to you." Abruptly she released Mary's hand and stood up, her black eyes looking intently into her face as she said, "I would know your name before I go."

"My name is Mary Campbell."

For the last time the Gypsy grasped Mary's right hand and traced on the palm two letters, R and B, saying, "This is the name of the one to whom you will be joined. He is your Destiny and no other. Your love will be as sweet as the budding rose, from which the petals never fall." So saying, she took Mary's left hand in hers, and bent low to touch it to her forehead, murmuring some words in her Romany tongue as she did so. Before they could gather their wits, the Gypsy had lifted her basket and vanished through the open door without a word of farewell. While the others discussed their fortunes and speculated on the truth of them or otherwise, Mary dreamed happily of Robert and their Betrothal, and gave no thought to the things she had not been promised, children and long years ahead.

When Jessie and Mary came out of Church that Sunday, they saw John Lees standing with what was obviously a family party – a pleasant faced, middle-aged lady, her son and young daughter. Mary heard Jessie gasp, "Losh sakes, it's Mistress Burns!" and at that, the hot blood rushed to her face and a fit of trembling seized her. Robert's Mother, here! She felt Jessie grip her arm and was glad of her support as they approached the watching group.

Not daring to lift her eyes, she heard John Lees say, "Good morning, ladies, may I present my friends? Mistress Burns, Mr Gilbert Burns, and Miss Isabella Burns; Mistress Jessie Smith and Miss Mary Campbell." Jessie and Mary dipped a respectful curtsey to the older woman, and Mary's fears vanished as she met her kindly gaze. While they chatted, Mrs Burns studied the tall, golden-haired girl, approving her simple dress with its modest white fichu, approving also her quiet unassuming manner. When they parted company, John Lees held back for a moment to slip a paper into Mary's hand, which she quickly placed in her purse, unseen by all but Jessie. In the kitchen of Montgomerie House, there was great excitement as they discussed Mary's meeting with Mrs Burns, but since it had been so brief and nothing of consequence had been said, they had to admit Jessie's verdict was true, that it had been purely a chance encounter.

In the privacy of her room, Mary opened out her letter and began to read.

Mary,

My Dearest Lass,

On the next Sabbath day, I will meet you on the banks of the Faile, beyond the bridge, beside the Stepping-stones. Come early, an hour before the Kirk bell, and bring with you a Bible, as an old Scottish tradition is that Bibles exchanged after vows over running water will bind us together as solemnly as any Sacrament, and such is my heartfelt wish. Until next Sabbath, dream of me, my true love, soon to be my Betrothed.

Your Ever-Loving Robert.

In the kitchen, Jessie moved about restlessly, banging dishes down with unnecessary force, wondering, would Mary never come? Surely she had finished reading her letter by now! Truth to tell, Jessie firmly believed that if Mary's fortune came true, then so too, would her own. To her relief, Mary came in to sit beside her, accepting the tea which Jessie poured for them both.

Gazing over her cup at the other's radiant face, she burst out, "Well, Mary, are you not going to tell me your news?"

Mary leaned over to touch her hand, saying softly, "Of course I will tell you, dear friend, and you only do I trust. Next Sabbath, I am to meet Robert by the Faile, and I am to bring a Bible. We are to make vows for our Betrothal, and later, we will be married in Campbeltown."

Jessie's eyes opened wide at this and she could hardly speak for excitement, "Why, Mary, that is just as the Gypsy told it! First your letter, then vows across water and three books exchanged!"

Mary looked doubtful and shook her head. "No,

Jessie, that is not so. It is only two Bibles, one from Robert and one from me. My Mother would say that telling Fortunes is a trick of the Devil, and not to be trusted."

Jessie was somewhat cast-down by this, but soon rallied and she argued, "How can you say that when you've seen it for yourself? What does it matter that she saw three books and you say two. She must have a gift to have seen so much!"

Not wanting to shatter Jessie's belief in the Gypsy's powers, Mary said no more, and soon forgot about Fortunes and Prophecies. Far more real to her were the days leading to her Betrothal, and after that the bright future belonged to her and Robert.

CHAPTER 22

Vows across the Faile

During the next week, Mary spent her every spare moment in preparation for her meeting with Robert. She added a new lace fichu and matching cuffs to her blue dress, then, placing them in the wooden chest, she sprinkled them with flowers of lavender before she closed the lid. "This will be my Betrothal," she told herself, "as sacred as my Wedding day, and I must greet Robert fittingly."

On the Sabbath morning, Mary awoke just before dawn, to find the room filled with a soft, golden glow. She heard the hesitant notes of the first birdsong, swelling to a joyous crescendo as others joined in. Leaning from the window, she saw the sun rise in all its splendour over the hills, lining them in brilliant gold. She breathed in the perfume from the purple lilac tree, and her heart beat with joy at the thought of Robert and their Betrothal. Swiftly she washed in cool rainwater and put on the fresh, white cotton garments she had laid out. She donned her second best dress, over which she fastened an all-enveloping white apron, and shaking Betty awake, ran lightly to the kitchen. When Jessie appeared, she found everything ready, the table set, porridge-pot bubbling from its hook over the red coals, kettle simmering on the hob.

Mary met her approving look with a smile, saying, "Such a lovely morning it was, I just had to get up and do something. It will help the time to pass till I go to meet Robert."

"You won't forget your Bible, will you?" Jessie asked anxiously. With a shake of her head, Mary assured her that such a thing was impossible, and as the others trooped in, no more was said. Long before the Church bell was due to ring out the service, Mary, dressed in her blue gown, was ready to be on her way. Jessie came into the room and watched as she placed one of her precious Bibles in her purse. In a sudden display of emotion, Jessie threw her arms around her and said, "Be happy, Mary lass, and may the sun always shine for you."

Taking her way along the green river-banks, Mary rejoiced in a feeling of freedom she had never before experienced. She sensed that her old life had ended, and that each step was taking her to a new life, so full of love it dazzled her mind as the sun overhead dazzled her eyes.

So it was that Robert Burns first saw her on that eventful Sabbath morning, appearing out of the sunlight, hair and face bathed in its golden rays. Eyes blinded, she shaded them and, seeing him come towards her, her smile shone with such radiance, the sun faded before it. He stepped forward to grasp the hands she held out to him, and raising them to his lips, kissed each one in turn, murmuring her name as he did so. His arm around her slender waist, he led her to a moss-covered log and seated her there, in a bower of sweet-scented briar roses.

Taking her hand, he gazed into her face, saying earnestly, "My dearest love, my Mary, this is our Betrothal day. Before we speak our vows, tell me now if you have any doubts in your heart, for, once we promise, there will be no going back."

Mary, fixing her eyes on his, gave her reply in a voice which did not falter. "Robert, my heart beats as your heart, so full of love there is no room in it for doubt. I do not wish, no, not ever, to go back, only to walk on with you by my side."

At this, his brown eyes glowing, he rose to his feet, drawing her with him, saying in a voice vibrant with happiness, "Then let us start our journey now, dear love of my life, without whom I have no life worth living." Hand-in-hand they walked along the flowering banks of the Faile, until they reached the Stepping-stones which spanned the narrowest crossing. Here they stopped and gazed at the sparkling water which was at its lowest ebb after the long hot spell. In silence, they listened to the gentle murmur of the stream, as it splashed and rippled over the peat-brown pebbles. Then, they turned to one another and exchanged a look both loving and solemn.

Mary listened carefully as Robert explained what was to happen, "I will cross the stream and face you from the other side. We both will lave our hands in the water and drink, then join hand to hand, and repeat our vows. I will say the words first, and you will reply with yours. After that, we seal those vows when we exchange our Bibles and I become your promised husband."

"And I, your promised wife," said Mary softly.

A moment longer they stood, hand-clasped, then Burns moved away and, sure-footed, stepped across the stones to stand on the opposite bank. Mary moved to the water's edge, facing him, and heard him say,

"Now, Mary, we lave our hands and drink."

They stooped to the stream and felt the coolness of the water as they cupped their hands to receive it, and savoured its coolness on their lips when they drank. Holding hands, he began, "I, Robert Burns, do pledge my Troth to Mary Campbell, and do solemnly promise to hold true to her, as my Betrothed, and as my Wife-to-be, for as long as we both shall live. This I do swear before God."

Her eyes on his, Mary spoke without faltering. "I, Mary Campbell, do pledge my Troth to Robert Burns, and do solemnly promise to hold true to him as my Betrothed, and as my Husband-to-be, for as long as we both shall live. This I do swear before God."

The moment seized and held them fast, and the scene imprinted itself on Mary's memory, never to be forgotten – the sparkling water, shining under the sunlight, Robert's face, so full of love, all appeared to her as a dream.

Then as he stepped to her side and enfolded her in his arms, the dream became reality. Bending his head, he stooped to kiss her lips and Mary's arms rose to cling around his neck. Gently, softly, they kissed, a kiss with nothing in it of passion, but one which lingered to put the seal on their Betrothal.

Standing together by the Faile, they began the ritual of exchanging their Bibles. To Mary's startled amazement, Burns produced not one, but two, small volumes, and she had a sudden quick memory of words spoken by the Gypsy, of three books to be given, but the thought vanished as swiftly as it had come.

Placing their hands over the Bibles, Burns spoke for both. "Oh Lord, we ask Thy Blessing on this, our Betrothal Day, and do swear on Thy Holy Book, to cleave, one to the other, for as long as we both shall live. Amen."

As these most solemn words died away, Mary felt a sense of exaltation and closed her eyes as she echoed Robert's "Amen." Receiving her two Bibles into her hand in exchange for her own, she heard Burns say earnestly,

"Mary, these are the most precious gifts we will ever possess, and for you, I have written in each one the words of a Text, which I have a wish to hear you read. But first, let us be seated."

Mary opened the Old Testament, in which was written her name, Mary Campbell, followed by a Text which she read out softly, "And ye shall not swear My Name falsely: I am the Lord. Leviticus XIX: 12." The New testament bore his own name, Robert Burns, and Mary read on, "Thou shalt not forswear thyself, but shall perform into the Lord thine oath. Matthew V: 33."

Now Burns opened the Bible which Mary had given him and looked at the words she had written: "May 1786. To Robert Burns from Mary Campbell. Our Betrothal Day. Ruth 1: 16, 17." Turning the pages to the Book of Ruth, he asked Mary to read the verses.

In her lilting, Highland voice, she spoke the beautiful words of Ruth to Naomi. "Intreat me not to leave thee, or to return from following after thee; for whither thou goest, I will go; and where thou lodgest, I will lodge; thy people shall be my people, and thy God my God: where thou diest, I will die, and there I will be buried: the Lord do so to me, and more also, if ought but death part thee and me."

Burns, deeply moved, asked, "Mary, lass, do you have the Gift of the Sight?"

Not understanding, she shook her head. "No, I think not. But why do you ask?"

"There is a thing I have been debating for some time, whether or not to make a new life for us in the Indies, but I feared to put the question and now, I no longer fear. Your words have answered me. But it is only a fancy of mine, nothing to trouble your mind."

The next hour flew past in tender caresses,

murmured endearments, and holdings, each to the other, in long, silent moments of blissful happiness. Burns knew that he should be telling Mary of his plans, but so deep in love was he that he refused to allow the world to come between them.

They were roused from their dreams by the swift, chattering flight of a bird close above them. Mary stirred, and lifted her head from Robert's shoulder, feeling his arms tighten around her as he whispered, "No, sweeting, not yet. Bide a while longer in my arms." Unresisting, she rested against him, as unwilling as he to end their moment of togetherness. Too soon, they made ready to leave the scene of their Betrothal. One last kiss, and the murmured words, one to the other, "I love you". Three words spoken by countless lovers through the ages, but to Mary and Robert, new-minted for them alone.

Before Burns took his leave of Mary, he to Mossgiel, she to Montgomerie House, it was understood that she would give in her notice and return to Campbeltown. As he put it, "I will sleep easier, Mary, if you are far away from Old Armour's spite, when I am not near to protect you. If he ever suspects we are betrothed, he'd hound me to Hell and back to prevent our Marriage, and would set the Kirk against us. For myself, I care nothing, but I'd not be responsible for my actions if they cast their vile insinuations against you!"

On her way back, passing the thorn tree, Mary paused to pick a fragrant cluster of creamy blossoms, recalling the carefree hours spent there with Robert. Then, he had been her dearest friend, and now he was her betrothed, her promised husband, beloved of her heart. As she walked on, she could feel the outline of her Bibles in her purse, as it swung from her wrist, and she wondered what Jessie would say when she learned that three books had been given. In the cool of the early evening, Jessie at last got Mary to herself, as they walked round the Herb garden, ostensibly picking fennel and mint, while making sure that there was no-one close enough to overhear them.

Jessie was first to speak, asking with a sideways glance, "Well, Mary, and are you now promised to Robert Burns?"

Blushing, shy and yet proud, Mary answered, "Yes, Jessie, we have made our vows, and when Robert is free to come to me, we will be married in Campbeltown. I am to give notice tomorrow and will leave at the end of the week."

Although she had half-expected this, Jessie experienced a sharp pang at the thought of losing her friend, but as she looked at Mary's radiant face, she put aside her own feelings and said warmly, "I'm so glad for you, for both of you, and I wish you happiness and joy in full measure."

It wasn't until they turned to go in, that Jessie suddenly asked, "But what about the Bibles, Mary? Were there only two?"

For a moment, Mary said nothing, then, reluctantly, she had to admit, "No, there were three. Robert gave me the Old and the New Testaments in exchange for the Bible I had for him." Jessie stood still, an odd look on her face which Mary did not understand.

When she spoke it was to say very quietly, "Aye, just as the Romany foretold." She had no words to describe her feelings, and no wish to cast shadows over Mary's happiness, so she turned a smiling face and said, "I am now admitting you were right, Mary. It was all a pottage of nonsense, made up of clever lies and superstition, to fool credulous folk like me!" Rewarded by seeing Mary's worried look change to bright happiness as they talked of her future with Robert, Jessie tried to put her own mind at rest. Much as she pinned her hopes on the future promised her by the Gypsy, she wished there had been only two Bibles, to prove her words wrong, and so dispel the nebulous cloud she had seemed to cast over Mary.

CHAPTER 23

Will ye go to the Indies?

O ne week and one day later, Mary was back in Campbeltown. Alone in her room, she tidied her hair and prepared to join her parents. She hoped that her Father had read Robert's letter, and not knowing exactly what it contained, she felt some anxiety as to his reactions. When she entered the bright kitchen where her parents sat, one to each side of the fireplace, she saw at once, from their smiling faces, that her fears were groundless.

Her Father held out his hand, and taking it, she seated herself beside him, as she had so often done as a child. Archie Campbell touched his daughter's cheek and asked, "Do you wish to read Robert's letter, Mary?"

She shook her head, "No, Father, but perhaps you would tell me what it says."

"Very well, lass, if that is your wish." Clearing his throat, he began.

> Dear Captain Campbell,
>   I respectfully request of you the greatest favour any Father could bestow, that is, the hand of your daughter, Mary, in Marriage.

Mary could not suppress her soft murmur of delight, which caused her Father to pause and brought a smile to her Mother's lips. If they had entertained any doubts as to her feelings, the happiness in her blushing face would have dispelled them.

After one keen glance, her Father continued.

> We have exchanged Betrothal vows, and though my circumstances at present are somewhat uncertain, I want you to know that I will always provide for Mary's welfare. It is our wish to be married in her Church in Campbeltown, and though I cannot set a precise date, it is my heartfelt hope that it will not be long delayed. I anxiously await your answer, for Mary's love is more to me than Life itself.

When Archie Campbell finished reading, Mary sat with downcast eyes, her heart touched by Robert's plea. Raising her gaze to her Father's face, she entreated him, wordlessly, to give his answer. Returning her look, he felt a sharp dart of mental anguish. He did not want to lose this best-loved child. To give her into the keeping of another man would, he knew, make her no less his daughter, but never again would he be first in her life. The moment passed, and he bent to kiss her forehead, telling her as he did so, "It is all right, Mary. My answer is yes, and tonight I will write to your Robert and tell him so."

Mary threw her arms around his neck, clinging to him as she whispered her thanks. Then she ran to her Mother and hid her face in her lap. Agnes Campbell between laughter and tears, raised Mary's face and kissed it soundly. To mark the occasion, Archie Campbell brought out his wife's Elder flower cordial, and for himself he poured a generous dram of fine old whisky.

One thing he felt bound to ask, and as they sipped their drinks, he came out with it. "Mary, does Robert truly believe in his Religion, or is it for him a thing of little importance?"

Colour flooded Mary's face as she looked into her Father's eyes. "Robert believes very strongly, Father, although he does not always reveal it. But wait you, and I will show you a thing which will tell you better than words of mine."

With this, she left the room, returning in a few moments with her Bibles, which she handed to her Father. "These were Robert's gift to me at our Betrothal, when I gave him my own Bible. I would like you to read the words he has written, and you also, Mother. Then you will have no more doubts." Her Father opened the Old Testament, and slowly read the verse that Burns had chosen. "And ye shall not swear My Name falsely: I am the Lord." In the New Testament, he pronounced the words with feeling, "Thou shalt not forswear thyself, but shall perform into the Lord thine oath." Silently, he passed the Bibles to his wife, and waited until she too had scanned the words.

Giving them back to Mary, Agnes Campbell looked to her husband, saying, "Well, Archie, I think we need have no doubts as to Robert's respect for God's Word, nor of his honourable intentions towards our daughter." With this, Archie Campbell wholeheartedly agreed, and promised Mary he would put no obstacle in the way of her Marriage to Robert Burns.

In the days that followed, Mary and her Mother spent much of their time filling Mary's Wedding Chest. They hemmed white linen for sheets and pillow-cases, crocheted woollen squares for blankets and stitched soft cotton and flannel for dusters and drying-cloths. For Mary, it was a labour of love, each stitch a part of her dream and that dream always of Robert and the home they would share.

On a lovely June day, a letter arrived for Mary, just as she was leaving on a visit to her sister Agnes, at a neighbouring farm. She decided to take her precious letter with her, to read on the way. This was her first news from Robert since their Betrothal, and it was with a feeling of relief that she turned aside from the main road into a lane lined with hedges of soft, green beech. Hidden from any passers-by, Mary sat down on the mossy bank and breathed a sigh of anticipation as she unfolded her letter. Immediately, his words seemed to leap at her from the page, evoking his very image and she could almost hear his voice.

Mary, dearest love of my life,

I picture your bonnie face as last I beheld it on our Betrothal day. That Sabbath is imprinted in my memory, a time never to be surpassed, though it will be equalled by our Wedding Day. Yes, my lovely lass, I have received your Father's consent and his Blessing, and it is balm to my soul to be welcomed into your Family. If only I could name the day, I would be the happiest man in the world, but I swear, hand on heart, it will not be too far distant.

While I wait (with very little patience) for your letter, I kiss your eyes, and your sweet red lips, and fit to each kiss the words "I love you" repeat them to me in your letter, my Mary, and never forget to 'say-me' in your

The Love of Highland Mary

Prayers. God bless and keep you till we
meet.

Your Robert.

Beneath his name, he had added a few words, "You have
my Heart, you have my Hand, to you I am in Honour
bound." Three times, Mary whispered, "I love you," as
if she were truly in his arms, as on their Betrothal day,
and she gave him back his words, "You have my Heart,
you have my Hand, to you I am in Honour bound."

At last, reluctantly, she folded away her letter and
resumed her journey. Soon, she was seated with her sister,
in the kitchen of Moor Farm, where she was served tea
and home-baked scones by the Cook. Looking at Agnes
as the three of them chatted together, Mary reflected on
her improved appearance. Her hair was neatly braided,
and her eyes shone, as she quietly conversed with a new
assurance. On leaving, Agnes accompanied Mary for part
of the way, and when she was told of her sister's Betrothal,
she smiled at her with genuine affection and wished her
happiness.

They stopped at the end of the path and Mary,
sensing a confidence witheld, asked, "Do you have a
special friend, Agnes?" Quickly the girl looked away, but
not before Mary saw the blood rush to her cheeks and
heard her say, "Well, there is Will, who walks with me to
Church. He is an apprentice Saddler and he is very nice,"
and with that she was gone.

Mary was glad that self-contained little Agnes was
happy, and hoped that Life would be kind to her. Then
she forgot her in dreams of Robert, resolving to thank
her Father for writing to him so warmly. She understood
what his acceptance meant to Robert after the bitterness
of his rejection by the Armours, restoring to him his self-

esteem, and healing his wounded pride.

When Captain Campbell returned home a few days later, he brought with him Mary's brother Rab, no longer 'Rab-the-Pirate' but a tall, handsome young man, with a mischievous twinkle in his dark eyes. When he saw Mary, he swung her up in the air and kissed her soundly on both cheeks, crying out, "And what's this our Father tells me? That you are to marry your Poet, Robert Burns? I declare it cannot be allowed, you are far too young!"

Blushing, laughing, Mary held him off. "It is 23 years I have, Rab, and see you, I am still your big sister!"

When young Archie came home from school, it was a happy family that gathered round the table, and after saying Grace, Mary's parents exchanged a silent look that gave thanks for their many Blessings, the greatest of which were their children. After the meal, when Mary and her Mother had cleared the table and washed the dishes, they carried their chairs outside to the garden. It was unusually warm for June, and they were glad of the cool, salt breeze that wafted in from the sea. Young Archie begged Rab to tell him a story of the great Ships that sailed into Greenock harbour, carrying cargoes of sugar for the Sugar Houses.

Rab was only too happy to oblige, and, turning to his young brother, he began, "Some of the Greenock streets are named after the islands where the sugar is grown, like Tobago Street, Jamaica Street, Antigua Street. When it's boiling in the factories, you can smell it all over the place, like burnt toffee. Just before I came away, some sailors came off a ship from Tobago. One of them, a native of the Island, was a giant, big as an ox, with gold earrings and the whitest teeth I've ever seen. It was his first voyage, and his shipmates took him to an Inn where he supped too much whisky and it went right to his head. He ran out into the street, bellowing and staggering, so that folk scattered away in a fine old panic. It took six Constables to get him into the Barrow and along to the Jail, where they locked him up in a cell for the night."

Here Rab paused for breath, and his Father shook his head at such on-goings, but Mary and her Mother expressed concern for the poor sailor, who surely hadn't meant any harm, and Archie urged Rab on to tell what had happened next.

"In the morning, he had to go before the Fiscal, and he was so hangdog, so sorry for his behaviour, he got off with a Fine. All his shipmates had a collection to pay for it, and took him back safely to his ship."

"Oh," breathed Archie, "I wish I could have seen him, but I'm awful glad his friends didn't leave him in that Jail!"

July broke hot and sultry, with overcast skies and quick, violent storms of thunder and forked lightning, during which time Mary wrote her letters to Robert and waited longingly for his replies. In his most recent message, he told her that he was working hard, and hoped that, by the end of the month, he would have delivered the last of his poems and songs to his Printer, John Wilson, in Kilmarnock. About his future plans, he wrote,

My friends advise me to leave the country, in order to thwart Armour's intentions.

Already the number of people who wish to purchase copies of my book, ensure it's success, and therein lies my danger. Armour is more than ever determined to have me arrested for non-payment of Maintenance, and has stirred up a Hornet's nest in the Kirk, so that I am Bedevilled on all sides. A good friend, Doctor Patrick Douglas of Ayr, has offered me a position on his Sugar estate in Jamaica, as Book-keeper, at £30 a year. The Contract is for three years and I am tempted to accept, if you will come with me as my Wife. I will write to your Father, whose judgement I value highly, and it may be that he will think it is all too sudden but there, everything could change overnight, except for one thing that will never change, Mary lass, my love for you and my determination to make you my Wife.

Mary, the thought of your steadfast love is a shining Light in the Darkness of all my Trials and Tribulations, the hardest to bear being my separation from the one I hold most dear, my Mary. For you, my lovely Dear, I would forego Fame, Fortune, aye, Heaven itself, for your sweet presence would make of my life a very Heaven on Earth.

Soon after, Archie Campbell received Burns's letter, and sat long deciding on his answer. At last, he joined Mary in the garden. His voice gentle, he told her he had given deep thought to Robert's request to be married so that she could go with him to Jamaica, as his wife. "But, lass, I do not think that is the right thing to do. Och, to be sure, I sympathise with his reasons, but I have the feeling that, if his book is a success, he might well have a change of heart and realise that his future is here, in his own land."

Mary watched the silver flight of a seabird, and considered her Father's words. "That is what would please me most, Father, but if Robert decides to go, what then?"

Archie Campbell met his daughter's gaze. "Well, then, I think it would be best if he went out on his own, to see if the life suits him, and if so, to get a home ready for you to join him. If you agree to this, I will write and tell Robert, but if it is going to make you too unhappy, then all I would ask is that he waits a while longer before taking you so far away from us."

Mary smiled up at him, recognising his anxiety and his deep love, and said, "Very well, Father, I will abide by whatever you and Robert think best." When Burns' answer came, Archie Campbell felt that a weight of anxiety had been lifted from his heart. He sensed Roberts indecision, realising that present circumstances had pressured him into accepting a solution which was expedient rather than desired, and breathed a heartfelt sigh of relief to know that he was agreeable to going out on his own to "get things ready for Mary".

Mary's letter, confirming what he had written to her Father, arrived the next day, telling her,

> I feel the sooner I set sail, the sooner I will be able to send for you, my own dear lass, to come to me and be my Wife.

Then, in the grip of strong emotion, his pen had pressed deeply into the paper, making a blot over her name.

> Mary, no words of mine can tell you of my anguish at having acceded to your Father's request! Of course, he is right, but my heart is sore-burdened at the thought of leaving you. If only I could be sure of my Book's success, not just here, in my own Scotland, but in the wider airts of the land, ah then,

nothing would drive me from you. It
comforts me to know the same stars shine
down from Heaven for you and for me, each
one a bright Star of Love, I kiss you as I love
you, with all my Heart.

> Your Loving, Longing,
> Robert.

Feeling his pain, sharing his loneliness, Mary's tears
overspilled, and she prayed God to sustain them both in
the days and nights that lay ahead. Other news came to
Mary, in a letter from Jessie Smith, telling her Jean
Armour had given birth to twins, a boy and a girl, on the
third of September, in the home of her Aunt in Paisley.

> And Effie's sister, Kirsty, says old Armour is
> just waiting to see if Rob will turn up to get a
> glimpse of the Bairns. But he will not, for he
> has been warned by his friends that the
> minute he shows his face, he'll be seized and
> clapped in Jail.

This news saddened Mary, offsetting the joy she had felt
on learning that Robert had postponed his journey to
Jamaica. People might think him unfeeling to make no
move towards his infants, but she knew differently. She
knew how much he cared for his little Bess, and how his
heart would yearn over his newborn twins.

By the end of September, the Campbell family
rejoiced to learn that Burns had given up all thought of
going to the Indies. Buoyed up by the runaway success
of his Book, and encouraged by the furore it had caused
in Literary circles in Edinburgh, he believed it would
enjoy an even greater success in the Capital than it had

in Ayrshire. He ended his letter to Mary's Father by telling him that, if a new edition of his book was published, it would bring him enough money to set himself up in a Farm and provide a secure future for Mary, "So that we could be married in the Spring of the year." At this news, Mary's cup of happiness overflowed. In her prayers that night, Mary had no requests to make, only thanks to give, that now they would not have to leave their Native land.

CHAPTER 24
Till Death us do Part

Late September in Broombrae was Autumn at its best, spilling golden sunshine over the landscape, with crisp, cool mornings and glittering, white-frosted nights.

Wrapped warmly in a dark blue cape, Mary drank in the splendour of the great Harvest moon, shining on the dark water and making on its sur face a broad path of gold. It was a night to be shared, and she longed for Robert's presence beside her until the ache in her heart became intolerable and she turned her back on the glistening scene and went indoors. Now that a time had been set for her Wedding in the Spring, it was decided that Mary would accept a well-paid position in Glasgow, in the household of a Colonel McIvor. Miss Elizabeth Campbell had arranged it, telling Mary that the money she earned would help to buy the many things needed to set-up house after her Marriage.

This was no sooner agreed, than other family events overlapped Mary's departure. Her brother, Rab, sent word that his Father and Mary were invited to his 'Brethering-Feast' at the beginning of October. The 'Feast' was to take place in the Greenock home of their Father's cousin, Peter McPherson, and his wife. They were to stay as long as they liked, and Mary could travel from Greenock to Glasgow to begin her new job at the end of October.

The Love of Highland Mary

As she packed her belongings, Mary faced a moment of indecision. Should she take her precious letters and Bibles with her? Or would they be safer here? Reluctantly, she decided to leave them where they were, until she returned to marry Robert. Moved by an inexplicable impulse, Mary rose and looked into the small mirror on the Dresser. Opening a drawer, she took out a pair of scissors, and cut a golden tress from her hair. Folding it over into a loop, she bound it with a silk thread and placed it carefully inside the cover of the Old Testament, murmuring the words over to herself, "And ye shall not swear by My Name falsely: I am the Lord."

Before she and her Father set sail, Mary gave her box of letters and Bibles into her Mother's hands, asking her to keep them safe till she returned. Then she added, "Mother, if anything should happen to me, you must promise to burn Robert's letters. I would not be wanting other eyes to read his love-words, they are for me alone."

When Agnes Campbell heard this, she felt a cold rippling of her skin, and a clutch of dread at her heart which she tried to laugh away, saying chidingly, "Why, lassie, you are only going away for a few months, and your things will be here when you come back."

Seeing the fear in her Mother's eyes, Mary smiled reassuringly. "Of course you are right, Mother. It is myself is over-anxious and see shadows where none exist. Was I not ever the same, even as a child?"

"Yes, indeed that is so, daughter. You were old for your years, as much a Mother as a sister to our wild laddie, 'Rab-the-Pirate'."

In their laughter at shared memories, fears were forgotten, and Mary's journey began in Autumn sunshine as she sailed with her Father to Greenock, on the River of Clyde. Waiting to greet them on the Harbour pier was

Rab, accompanied by Peter McPherson, a broad-shouldered, ginger-haired man of some forty-five years.

Introduced to Mary, he claimed a Kinsman's right to a hearty kiss on each cheek, before holding her off to look at her admiringly, saying, "Aye, Rab, ye didnae tell me your sister was sic' a bonnie lass!" Archie Campbell cleared his throat, none too pleased at McPherson's familiarity, which had brought a crimson blush to Mary's face. Shrewdly reading the situation, Peter McPherson released Mary and reached out to grasp his cousin's hand in a crushing grip. He bid him welcome to Greenock, and taking him by the arm, led the way onto the busy main street, leaving Rab to follow with Mary.

Mary was both fascinated and repelled by the sights that met her eyes. Well-dressed ladies and gentlemen rubbed shoulders with shawl-draped women and drunk men; horse drawn carts and carriages rumbled over the cobblestones, scattering filth from the gutters over the crowds, who yelled imprecations in words Mary did not understand. The sky was obscured by tall tenements, and an offensive stench mingled with a dank mist that drifted in patches over the streets.

Glad of Rab's supporting arm, Mary held a handkerchief over her face, breathing in the clean smell of lavender and gasping, "Rab, I know you told us about the terrible conditions in the town, but never, never did I dream it was anything like this. How can you stand to live here?"

"Och, you get used to it after a while, and I spend my days in the Yard, right beside the River, where you can smell the seaweed and watch the big ships sailing in and out."

To Mary's relief, they left the noisy, crowded main street and turned into a quieter area of small, two-storied houses. In front of one of these, McPherson stopped, and waited for them to catch up as he said, "Welcome to Charles Street, Mary, home of the McPherson's and your home for as long as you will bide."

Mary looked at a curved iron-railed stair which led up to the second floor, and McPherson, following her gaze, told her, "Aye, that's part of our house, lass. Two rooms up, two down."

As he spoke the street door was flung open and a small, stout woman, red-cheeked and black-haired, darted out, loudly scolding her husband, "Shame on you, Peter McPherson, keeping our guests waiting on the door step!" Standing on tiptoes, she reached up to plant a warm kiss on Mary's cheek. "My, you're awful like your Mother! A right bonnie lassie."

Turning to Rab, she instructed him, "You, Rab, take your sister's bag up to the Bird room," and to a mystified Mary, as she led her inside, "You and me, we are going to sleep up the stairs and the men will bed down here – that's if anybody gets to lie-down this night!"

All the space in the kitchen was taken up by a long, trestle table, with benches on either side. A blazing fire burned red in the shining range and the heat was stifling. Mary was glad to remove her cloak and hang it on the peg behind the door. Mrs McPherson, or Cousin Jean, as she told Mary to call her, lifted the boiling kettle from the hob, and poured the water into the waiting teapot, while Mary and the three men sat down at the table. Jean had baked a score of mutton pies and urged everyone to "eat hearty" to stave off hunger until the guests arrived at seven o'clock. Mary admired the Teapot, a handsome piece, decorated with blue and gold flowers and birds, and was told it was part of a Tea-set that Peter had ordered from a Ship's Captain, all the way from China.

She looked at Mary and said, "Rab tells us you are to be wed soon, to Robert Burns the Poet, from Ayrshire. Have you fixed a date yet?"

Blushing, Mary shook her head. "Not exactly, Cousin Jean, but it will be in the Spring of next year."

"Well, lassie, that's not so long to wait, and I have the very thing upstairs for your Wedding Gift. I'll show it to you later."

Mary's face brightened with pleasure as she said, "It will be our very first Marriage Gift, so always it will be special to Robert and me."

Peter McPherson laughed as he warned her, "Better wait and see what it is first, Mary lass! You might not like it at all, at all!" But Mary shook her head, knowing it would please her no matter what it turned out to be.

Before the guests arived, Rab took Mary up to see her room. He pointed to a glass case containing some stuffed birds, a pair of pheasants with eggs, an owl with round, glass eyes on a branch, a blackbird and a robin. There was something so unnatural about their dead eyes that Mary shivered with revulsion, and she was glad that her narrow bed was separated from the case by a large chest-of-drawers, on which stood a jug of water, a basin, and a folded towel. The sound of people arriving drifted up to them, and Jean's voice summoned them to come down and meet everyone.

In the kitchen, Mary found herself engulfed in a sea of strangers, her senses reeling under the onslaught of loud voices and the rich smell of food and drink, and she wished only to be back in Broombrae under the quiet sky. Rab was the Hero of the hour, and he was toasted over and over again as a new 'Brother' of the Shipbuilding craft. Archie Campbell was proud of his son's ability to reply with eloquent speeches to the many compliments that came his way, though his ready tongue got a little tangled up as the night wore on.

In the early morning hours, when the merriment showed no signs of abating, Mary slipped out and climbed the stairs to her room. Thankfully she got into bed, so tired that she fell asleep before her prayers were properly finished. She awoke to darkness, caused by the fog that coated the glass panes of the tightly shut window. Aware of the strangeness of the room, Mary avoided looking over at the birds in their case. She was glad when Cousin Jean came in to light the candles and hurriedly washed and dressed before hastening down to the kitchen. To her surprise it was empty, the table cleared, the dishes piled in the sink.

Jean explained that the men had gone to the Yard and her Father to his boat. Laughingly, she said, "Aye, there will be a lot of sore heads when the hammers ring out this day! I'm thinking it is your Father has the best o' it!" As they drank their tea and ate hot, buttered bannocks, Jean McPherson wanted to know all about the job Mary was going to, and when she would see her Robert.

Mary explained that one of her reasons for taking the position was that it would be easier for Robert to visit her in Glasgow, adding that Colonel McIvor was interested in helping with his Book of Poems. Jean was astounded to learn that the couple had not met since their Betrothal in May, exclaiming, "Then it is just as well that you will see more of each other after this month, and soon enough you'll be planning your Wedding. And that reminds me of your Gift. Sit you still while I fetch it."

In a few moments she was back, holding a square wooden box which she placed carefully on the table.

Removing a pad of straw, she set out cups and saucers, so fine they were translucent. They were of the same design as the teapot, with little figures as well as flowers and birds in rich colours of crimson, blue and gold.

Mary gasped with delight, and gently lifted a cup so that the glow of the fire shone through it. "Cousin Jean, never have I seen anything so lovely. I cannot thank you enough. Indeed, I do not know how to thank you at all!"

Jean, well pleased, was a typical Scot who, distrusting any show of emotion, said brusquely, "Och, it's nothing, just a wee minding. I have another half-set left."

As she helped Jean with the chores, Mary's head was full of happy dreams, as she pictured setting out her Wedding china for her very first meal with Robert. When the men came home from the Yard, Peter McPherson was in high good humour, obviously suffering no ill-effects from his social evening as he ate his meal with obvious relish. The same could not be said of Rab, who, flushed and heavy-eyed, picked at his food while swallowing very little. He drank thirstily from the water-jug, filling his glass and gulping it down to ease an aching throat. Mary watched him with growing concern, and when she urged him to lie down, her concern turned to alarm when he obediently did as he was told.

As soon as he was in bed, Mary bent over him, laying her cool hand on his burning forehead, observing his over-bright eyes and the restless tossing of his head on the pillow. Peter and Jean McPherson came to see how Rab was feeling, and looking at his flushed face and bloodshot eyes, Peter's face sobered, as did his wife's.

Mary looked from one to the other in mounting alarm. "What is it? What is wrong with Rab?"

It was Jean, who, drawing Mary out of the room, told her, "Now, now, lassie, dinnae fret yourself. It looks like the lad's got a wee touch o' the Greenock Fever. You'd best leave his nursing to me and Peter, for we've both had it and won't take it twice."

Mary looked at her gratefully, but shook her head, saying, "It is very kind of you, Cousin Jean, but I will be easier in myself if I am always close at hand. Rab knows me, and will be less fretful if he hears my voice. And so, in the next few days, Mary nursed her brother through his illness. She wrung out wet cloths for his burning forehead, cloths which dried instantly so high was his temperature. She saw to it he had constant glasses of boiled water to drink, and held his hand while he tossed on the bed and reverted to scenes of his childhood. Mary's eyes filled with tears as her brother's hoarse voice brought back to her happy days in Dunoon.

Suddenly he sat bolt upright, crying, "Race you to the Baugie Burn, Mary!" and tried to get out of bed. Only with the help of Peter-McPherson was she able to get him back under the blankets, gentling him with soothing words and cool hands. When he at last fell silent, Mary feared the worst, but McPherson reassured her.

"It's all right, lassie, the fever's broken. He'll sleep now, and come the morning, he'll be ready for his food." Mary felt an intolerable burden lifted from her heart when Peter's words proved true, and within the week, Rab was well enough to accompany his Father to Campbeltown and ordered by McPherson not to return till he was "fighting fit". Before he left, Rab held Mary close for a long moment, pressing his cheek to hers before saying, with a new maturity, "You have seen the last of 'Rab-the-Pirate', Mary. From now on, I am Rab, the brother whose life you gave back to him."

In these few words, Mary was repaid in full measure, and with deep thankfulness for his recovery, she waved him goodbye. Next day, the hanging mists disappeared from the streets, and the sun came out to gild roofs and chimneys, so that they shone against the pale blue sky.

Jean McPherson, looking at Mary's drooping figure and heavy eyes, told her, "You're tired out, my girl, that's what is ailing you. You need some fresh air, and so do I. So go and put on your bonnet and cloak and I'll show you that Greenock isn't all herrings and smoke and bad smells. On a day like this it can look right bonnie."

Going down Charles Street, she pointed out the Royal Close, where the herrings were packed in barrels of brine to be shipped out to Europe and Russia. "And that long, narrow lane is the Vennel. Would you like to take a look?"

Mary shook her head, desiring only to get away from the crowds. She breathed a sigh of relief when they turned up a steep hill, called by Jean 'Schaw's Brae' and when they reached the top, she was astonished to see a fine Mansion House surrounded by green lawns and gardens.

Panting a little after her climb, Jean said, "It is more than a hundred years old, built by the Laird of Greenock, John Schaw, for his wife, Helen Houston. Aye, and there's a fine Well with their initials, full of sweet water, no like the stuff we have to drink down the hill."

On this bright Autumn morning the view over the River Clyde to the Argyllshire Hills and Bens, was a scene to take the breath away, and Mary feasted her eyes on its beauty, while filling her lungs with the cold, invigorating air. She reflected that this was indeed a different aspect of the dirty, clamorous streets of the town, and for a while she was able to forget her feeling of malaise. The fine weather did not last, and was followed by sea-mists which seeped through closed windows and dimmed even the brightest of fires. Mary's lassitude did not get any better, and Jean McPherson regarded her with worried eyes.

That next morning, she made her stay in bed, and brought her a cup of hot milk with butter and brown sugar melted in it, but after a few sips, Mary put it aside, and closing her eyes, lay back on the pillow. Thinking it better to let her sleep, Jean tip-toed quietly out of the room.

But Mary was not asleep, she was burning up with fever, which changed to icy chills that wracked her whole body in convulsive spasms. When at last the fever and the shivering ceased, Mary was left in a state of exhaustion. She was dimly aware of Jean bathing her forehead, and removing her drenched nightgown, and she moaned softly in relief as she was rubbed down with a warm towel and enveloped in a dry robe. Lastly, Jean combed out the long, golden hair, braiding it in a plait to hang down her back.

Only half-conscious, Mary did not know that many of Jean's friends came to ask after her, bringing with them a variety of remedies. One of these was a polished black stone found in a stream in the old Kirkyard, to be placed in a glass of boiled milk and drunk at midnight. Others consisted of concoctions of herbs, to be infused and taken every half- hour to kill the fever.

But all were to no avail, and Mary grew gradually weaker. Tossing in a fresh onset of delirium, Mary was back with Robert Burns on the banks of the Faile. She felt the rippling water flow over her wrists as she dipped her hands in the cool depths, before reaching them out to be enfolded in Robert's firm grasp.

Jean McPherson coming into the room, was halted by the sound of Mary's voice, low and clear, saying, "I, Mary Campbell, do pledge my troth to Robert Burns, and do solemnly promise to hold true to him as my

Betrothed and as my Husband-to-be, for as long as we both shall live. This I do swear before God."

Jean realised with dread, that Mary's shining blue eyes were fixed on a scene far removed from this room, and that her illness was reaching a critical stage. Almost despairingly, she applied cold compresses to Mary's burning forehead, soothing her as she would a sick child, while listening to her quote words from the Bible.

"Thou shalt not forswear thyself, but shall perform into the Lord thine oath." After these words, Mary lapsed into silence, staring at the window with blank unseeing eyes. Jean, sitting by the bedside, wished fervently that her husband would come home, so that she could send him for the Doctor, even though the medicine he had prescribed had done no good. He had told Peter there was an epidemic of Typhoid fever, the most virulent strain, for which there was no effective cure. Some might survive, most did not.

Brooding, watching fearfully over this girl she had come to love as her own. Jean McPherson saw a great calm come over Mary, smoothing the pain from her face and lighting it with a radiance not of this world, as she smiled, reached out her hands and said in a voice full of love, 'Robert', before the light went out forever.